BLIND DATE

BELLA JEWEL

St. Martin's Paperbacks

BLIND DATE

Copyright © 2017 by Bella Jewel.

All rights reserved.

For information address St. Martin's Press, 175 Fifth Avenue, New York, NY 10010.

ISBN: 978-1-250-10836-4

Our books may be purchased in bulk for promotional, educational, or business use. Please contact your local bookseller or the Macmillan Corporate and Premium Sales Department at 1-800-221-7945, ext. 5442, or by e-mail at MacmillanSpecialMarkets@macmillan.com.

Printed in the United States of America

St. Martin's Paperbacks edition / August 2017

St. Martin's Paperbacks are published by St. Martin's Press, 175 Fifth Avenue, New York, NY 10010.

10 9 8 7 6 5 4 3 2 1

PROLOGUE

"I miss you, Ray." I see her lips mouth a touching tribute to her husband as she places a bright bunch of flowers by his headstone.

My eyes zone in on her—small but strong, kneeling near a puddle of water as she runs her fingers over the stone. Her mousy brown hair is tucked neatly at the nape of her neck, pinned with a black clip. I wonder if she did that herself? Maybe her friend did, the one standing to her left, staring down at her with a soft look on her face.

My heart flickers.

But it isn't out of pity for the girl. No, it's pure joy. She's unlike anything I've ever seen before, unlike anything I've ever had experience with. I've been watching her for a while. All the rest—their situations were different. But this one . . . she's strong willed. I can see it in the way she clenches her fists, stopping herself from breaking down. She isn't the kind to fall to her knees and scream. She's stronger than that. It's written all over her, right down to the hard set of her jaw as she holds herself back from crying.

No. She's not like the weak-willed women I've played with in the past.

I can feel it in my chest—she is the one. She is the goal, the ultimate prize. I can't rush with her. No, I have to take this slow; break her into tiny little pieces before I attack. I need to do my research and get this right. She isn't going to be easy, but she's going to be worth it. She is going to be the one I remember forever; I can feel it right down into my bones.

Yes. She's what I've practiced so hard for.

I'll have to change up my game. I can't do this the way I've done it with all the other women. This one is special and deserves special treatment. She's going to get everything that I've got bottled up inside for all this time. I'm going to play this one differently and make this girl my trophy. I'm going to swoop into her life like a hurricane, only she won't be able to see me. She'll feel me though.

I'll be back for her.

She'll never know what hit her.

Hartley Watson.

I'm coming for you.

ONE

Hartley

"C'mon, Hart, it's been four years. You can't keep hiding away, avoiding the world."

I glance at Taylor, my best friend and a royal pain in my ass, and grimace. "Maybe so, but going on a blind date hardly seems like the ideal situation to get back out there. I've read about those—they never end well."

Taylor raises a pretty blonde brow; even giving me a sarcastic expression she looks gorgeous. Blonde, tall, lean, and fit. She doesn't need to worry about finding a date—she has them lining up. "How would you know? You've never been on one. You were with Raymond for ten years. When was the last time you even knew what it was like to meet a new person?"

The mention of my husband's name has my chest constricting, though it's not as bad as it used to be. During those first few years after I lost him in a car accident, there was a stabbing pain every living, breathing moment. I don't think I went a day without that pain cutting through me. But over time, it turned into a slow ache—some days bad, some days barely there, but always a constant, in one way or another. A continuous reminder that he's gone, and that I'm still here without him. At least I can wake up without tears running down my cheeks now. That was a big step.

That was when I first felt like I was finally healing. That was six months ago.

"I don't want to meet any new people." I shrug. "Not by forcing it, anyway. It seems wrong . . ."

Taylor keeps that eyebrow raised, and crosses her arms, causing the purple blouse she's wearing to crumple up at the front. "Look, honey, I know you might not want to be ready, or even want to think about it, but it can't hurt to go on a date. It's not like you have to marry the guy. You have a few drinks and if you don't like him, you leave and never have to see him again."

I study her for a moment. She's stubborn. She doesn't budge when she gets an idea in her head. Those hazel eyes hold mine without hesitation, without even flickering in a different direction. She won't back down, and I damn well know it. When Taylor is in one of her life-changing moods, nobody can tell her no. Nobody.

"You're not going to let this go, are you?" I mumble, turning my attention away and squinting as I try to feed a piece of thread through a needle so I can sew a button onto my favorite green blouse, which I've probably far outworn but can't part with. It's comfortable, so incredibly comfortable. And it was the last thing I wore when Raymond was alive. The last thing he touched. The last thing he saw me in.

Taylor makes a little sound in her throat, bringing my full attention back. "Hart, you're young and you could be out there, getting all the love you deserve. Can you just do this for me? Please? Go on a few dates, and if you hate them I swear I'll never ever mention it again. I'll leave you to sew buttons and stay huddled up in this apartment for another four years, wasting away."

I give her a foul look, and she blinks innocently at me.

Damn her. She's good. She knows how to push my buttons and get beneath the surface to stir me up and get what she wants. We've known each other too long—that's the problem. She might as well be my sister, my other half, basically a part of me. And she can read me like a damned book.

"One," I say, looking back down to feed the needle through the button and then through the material of my blouse. "One date, and that's it."

"Five."

I snort. "One."

"Four dates. C'mon, Hartley."

She puts her hands together in a pleading gesture, those big eyelashes batting as she looks at me like some sort of desperate kitten.

I narrow my eyes at her. "Two."

"Three and we'll call it even."

I sigh. "I don't know why I have to go out with three men. Can't I just go out on one date and be done with it? I'm not interested in seeing anyone. I'm not sure I'll ever be interested in dating anyone again. Honestly."

She's already smiling way too big, because she knows she's won. She knows it and she's thrilled with it. "You don't know until you try, and hey, you might even just find a friend out of it. Wouldn't it be nice to have a friend at the very least?"

I squint at her again. "Last time I checked, that's what you are."

She smiles prettily. "Yes, but I mean a male friend. One who might make you laugh. Who might make you feel good again."

"You do all of that," I mumble, putting the needle between my lips as I adjust the button. I know what she means but I'm not going to give her the satisfaction of admitting it.

"Stop arguing with me, and just do as you're told."

I giggle, and the needle drops from my lips. I know what she's doing, and I know it's probably time I give in and start getting back out there, but the very idea of dressing up and going on a date makes me cringe. I don't think it's because I don't want to. I mean sure, one day I do want to meet someone, I guess it's just the fear of being that . . . open with someone again.

I never really dated Ray. We met through mutual friends when we were in our early twenties and we just sort of starting talking—he made me laugh, I'll always remember that. During our first conversation, he had me in hysterics. One thing led to another and before I knew it, we were together. Sure, we went out after that, but there was never the awkward first date moment, where the possibility of getting stuck with a stranger for at least an hour is high.

Then there is the issue of trying to figure out something to say. I groan inwardly, honestly not sure I'm cut out for this. I've never been good with new people, let alone small talk, but Taylor is right, it has been four years and I've held myself back. I can't do that forever. So maybe enduring a few dates is, at the very least, a step in the right direction. I don't want to be alone forever—I truly don't— but I won't deny that the idea of stepping back into the terrifying world of dating does frighten me a little.

"Fine," I give in, and sigh. "Three, but that's it. When it doesn't work out with any of them, and it likely won't, then you leave me alone and mention nothing of the male species again."

She claps her hands together. "It's a deal, but you have to at least try. I don't want to hear you showed up on your worst behavior and ruined things before the men even got to say a word."

I huff. "You just ruined my plan. I was going to wear my ugliest jeans, and dribble while I ate."

She slaps my arm as I grin up at her.

"Don't be smart, Hartley. Trust me, this is going to be good for you."

I grunt. It'll definitely be *something* for me, but whether "good" is the word I'd use is to be determined. "Where, dare I ask, are you going to find these three eligible bachelors?"

She grins mischievously and rubs her hands together. I don't want to hear her answer, not when she's giving me a look that screams she's been up to no good. "I've already found them."

She. *Wait . . . what*? How in the hell could she have found three men, in such a short time?

"Taylor!"

She puts her hands up in self-defense as I throw

the nearest item at her, which happens to be a roll of thread. It bounces off her shoulder and trails across the floor, leaving a long line of string in its wake. Great. That'll take forever to roll back up.

"Come on, you didn't think I would get you to agree without having this all ready to go, did you?"

I scowl at her. That's exactly what I thought. I figured I had at least a few weeks or maybe she'd move on to something else and forget about it entirely. Besides, where in the hell does she get time to find three men for me, as well as work, and basically attempt to run my entire life?

She rolls her eyes. "Stop scowling, Hart. You need to start using that beautiful smile to attract these gorgeous prospects."

I roll my eyes right back. "Where did you find three men?"

"I found five, actually, but I can narrow them down to three. And there is this singles website, it's actually called **blind date**. It's really super cool. You put in all your details—what you're interested in, right down to the way someone looks—and it sends you matches. You ask them for a date, they agree or disagree. If they agree, you set up a location and meet. It's kind of mysterious, don't you think?"

I wouldn't go as far as "mysterious," but I can think of at least ten ways that could go wrong. I mean seriously, it's like a website created for all the crazies of the world to lie and then to meet on dates. I don't know how the creator thought it would be a successful idea. Although, obviously it *is* successful because Taylor has found me not one, not two, but five men. Thank God I only agreed to three. "If

I get sold as a sex slave, it's all your fault," I say, wagging my finger at her.

She laughs. "Don't be so dramatic. You're far too mouthy for that. They'd sooner chop you into a thousand pieces before using you as a slave—you'd drive them crazy in a day."

I flip her the bird, and she winks at me.

"The first date is tonight, by the way. I have a dress for you."

My eyes pop wide open. She's kidding, no? Tonight? My heart clenches in a strange way—nerves, maybe? It's been so long since I've felt anything even remotely like the anxious feeling bubbling in my tummy. Am I truly ready for this? I guess I'm not getting much of a choice. "Taylor, seriously . . ."

"You're welcome."

I pout at her. "There will be revenge for this. Sweet, sweet revenge."

"Yeah, yeah." She flicks a hand dismissively. "You better finish sewing on that button, because we need to find you some shoes to wear—oh, and some jewelry."

I haven't been on a date in over ten years. I'm nearly thirty-four. That's a big gap. A lot has changed since I was twenty-four. Am I even what men are looking for these days? What is the norm for a woman? Should I be blonder? Thinner? I wouldn't even know what to talk about. Will it be awkward? What if I hate the person and can't escape? This isn't the traditional way of meeting someone, and that makes me nervous.

Suck it up, Hartley. Eventually, it has to happen.

"What's going to happen if I don't like the guy, like I mean really don't like him?" I ask.

She nods, like she's got every scenario figured out well in advance. "Simple. You send me a text, and I'll call you pretending to be your pregnant sister who has just gone into labor."

"Not original at all." I roll my eyes.

She shrugs. "Well, it'll work. Now, let's find something we can do with your hair."

I pout. "Do I really have to do this?"

She crosses her arms. "If you ever want to be left alone, yes."

I grind my teeth. "And this is the only option?"

"You could always go and ask that gorgeous neighbor of yours."

I raise my brows. "Ace?"

"Mmmmhmmm. He's fine. I'd tap that all the way out of this apartment building."

I laugh. "Ace is a dick. He won't even say hello to me when I wave. He's so . . . brutal. Seriously."

She shrugs again. "He's a cop. That's what they do."

I raise a brow, like that explanation is supposed to let him walk around thinking he's better than the rest of the world. Manners should be a part of everyday life, no matter what your profession is. "He's a detective, actually, and manners aren't exactly hard. Surely he has to deal with people in his everyday life. I mean how hard is it to say hello?"

"Maybe he didn't hear you," Taylor offers, quirking a brow.

"Oh, he hears me. I waved right in his face once, and he just stared at me."

She wiggles her brows. "Well, the silent types usually have a wild side beneath the surface. You could skip past all the dating and just go right in there for the time of your life. Maybe that's all you need."

I snort. "No thank you. I'd sooner poke my eye out then hit Ace up for anything."

She laughs. "He is hot though. Even you have to admit that."

Ace Henderson—detective, jerk, and moody asshole—lives right next door to me. He has that tall, dark, handsome, broody thing going on. Yes, Ace Henderson is fine. Any woman with two eyes and a beating heart would admit that.

He's also a prick.

"I never said he wasn't easy on the eyes, but no. Let's stick to your blind dates."

Taylor claps her hands together. "I'm so excited."

Lord help me.

This is a bad idea.

A really bad idea.

I should turn around and go home, right now, before this random stranger arrives. Maybe I can fake a stomachache, to keep Taylor off my back. I don't know what I was thinking. This could go wrong on so many levels. I don't know if I'm ready to meet another man, even if it is just to be friends. I fidget and stand awkwardly out front of the restaurant-slash-bar. I try to look inconspicuous, but I'm sure I stand out like a sore thumb.

The wind tickles my cheeks, calming me down. I focus on the couples sitting at the large outdoor tables, covered by big black umbrellas, and I feel at ease. It'll be okay. It will be great.

My phone buzzes in my purse, distracting the crazy mess of thoughts in my head, and with fumbling fingers

I pull it out, seeing a text from Taylor flashing on the screen.

> T: Don't even think about running, and no, your excuses will not work. This will be good for you.

Damn her.
She's a mind reader.

> H: I hate you. If this date is a creeper, you're going to pay.
> T: Love you!

Shaking my head, I tuck my phone back in my purse just as a smooth voice says, "Hartley?"

It's a nice voice. Masculine, thick and deep. I exhale, feeling a little better. I'm being overdramatic, I know this. I need to get myself together and relax. I won't enjoy myself if I'm wound up this tight. So I turn and gaze at the man behind me.

It takes all my strength to hold in my gasp.

For a few moments, I just stare. I'm not a judgmental person. I don't take people on face value and I'm certainly not shallow, but this man is a good fifteen years older than me. Taylor briefed me on this date, telling me Greg was only five years older than I was, so I know right off the bat he has lied.

I think that's what shocks me the most. Not that he's not my type, but that he lied. What else did he lie about?

This doesn't make me feel secure. At all.

In front of me is a man, *well* into his forties, with a balding head and not much else going for him. His sky blue eyes are surrounded by bushy brows, and he's slightly overweight, which shows in both his body and in his rounding face. He's wearing a pair of clean black slacks and a button-up gray shirt. At least he's well dressed.

"Ah," I finally squeak, trying to control my shock and find my manners. "Yes."

"I'm Greg."

Greg.

Don't be judgmental, Hartley. That's a fine name. At least he didn't lie about that. He's probably a really nice man, even if his smooth, masculine, sexy voice does not match him. At all. How does that happen? How can his voice scream sex god and be so completely off? God. What am I doing? I'm being a terrible person. I haven't even had a conversation with the man.

Perhaps he could make a good friend.

Yes. A good friend. There. I feel better now.

Kind of.

"Hi, Greg," I say, exhaling the breath I was holding in my lungs.

It was starting to hurt.

He smiles sheepishly, showing his straight white teeth. He seems like a nice guy, and my guard drops just a little. He's probably just nervous like I was, so I should go easy on him. "Look, before we go on, I'm sorry I don't really fit the description I listed on my profile. It's just really hard to find a date these days, people judge someone before they even meet them. I know I wasn't completely honest."

I'm that person.

Judgy bitch.

I need to give myself a solid talking to. I didn't even want to go on a date and now that I'm here I am judging this man because he's caught me off guard. I've barely let the man speak and I've already dismissed him. That's unfair.

I smile, even though I'm still a little uncomfortable. But it would be unfair not to at least have a drink with him. It won't take long, it's polite—the right thing to do, even. "Do you want to go inside and get a drink?"

He seems to relax a little. "Of course. After you."

I turn and walk into the bar, letting Greg follow behind. He's a little too close for comfort, but I don't say anything. I just sit down on a barstool, and he takes the one directly next to mine. If I study him, really look, I can see that in his younger days, he was probably a nice-looking man. Maybe even enough to match that voice. But age has clearly caught up with him. It seems like he's spent a lot of time in the sun, which has probably prematurely aged him.

But I'm still thinking he may be closer to fifty. Unfortunately, no matter how great of a guy he may turn out to be, I know it won't work. I really don't think I can get over the age difference. I can do friends. Yes, friends. God, I'm going to kill Taylor. Kill her, and then bury her body in a shallow grave. Something completely unclassy.

But, if I'm going to get back into dating, I need to practice being in these types of situations. Besides, I wouldn't want someone to be rude to me if I wasn't their type. It's nerve-racking enough to be on a date, let alone to be rejected. I'm not that cruel. I can make conversation. I can be friendly. At least I'm out of the house, right?

"So what brings a beautiful girl like you to a dating site?" Greg asks me.

"I lost my husband four years ago, and I wanted to get back out there again, I guess."

To give him credit, Greg doesn't flinch, freak out, or take a staggering step back at the news that I lost my husband. I've not had many men try to talk to me since I lost Raymond, but the few that have seem to lose interest quickly when I mention that I'm a widow. I don't understand why, but it's like something in their minds just switches off and they do an instant retreat. Greg's eyes soften as he says, "I'm sorry to hear that. That must have been very difficult."

See? He's a nice guy.

I smile, and relax my shoulders just a touch, trying to take deep breaths and get comfortable. I realize I'm nervous, regardless of my lack of attraction to Greg. "Thank you. What about you, Greg? What brings you into the dating world?"

He shrugs and holds my eyes with his. "I just want to meet someone, get my life together. I don't want to spend the rest of my life living alone. I'd like a family. The universe wasn't presenting someone to me, so I figured I'd take a step and see what was out there."

Aw. He's kind and he seems smart. I don't know why he would have to lie to get a date. I'm sure there are plenty of lovely women out there in his age range who would like a chance with someone like him.

"That's a good goal to have."

This still feels a little awkward. If Greg notices, he certainly doesn't show it. His posture is relaxed, he's got an easy smile on his face, and he's sipping his drink like he's quite comfortable.

"Yes, I think so too," he continues. "I've been on a few dates, but all the women in my age range just aren't up to my standard. So I'm finding it really hard to find someone to connect with, you know?"

Silence.

Dead silence.

I blink.

Did he just say not up to his standard?

"Not that I'm picky," he says quickly, clearly seeing the horrified look I just presented him with. "But I just have a type. It's hard when you know what you want, but have to twist things around to get it. I don't want to come across as sleazy. We all have a picture in our mind, don't you think?"

I blink again.

He's kidding me, right?

No. I must be reading him wrong. Surely he did not just say those words and mean them. I must be misunderstanding him. Because, if I'm not, it all suddenly makes sense. The lying in his profile. How comfortable he is around me, considering his age. No. I must be wrong.

"And your picture is?" I ask, my voice a little horrified.

He looks sheepish. "I prefer someone younger than myself, pretty is a must, slim in build, funny, stable job. Just the usual things a man looks for. You don't think that makes me shallow, do you?"

Yes.

Yes I freaking do. I'm horrified. If he had just said he wants a successful woman, no problem. Or a funny woman, totally okay. But a young, skinny, pretty woman . . . not okay. Never okay. That is bordering on shallow, and I don't appreciate shallow men. And here I thought I was being superficial when I first saw him. That was nothing compared to him.

Swallowing the insult I want to throw at him, I say through gritted teeth, "There are plenty of lovely, pretty women in your age range though, right?"

His eyes dart to the left, then back to mine. "Yes, but as I said, I prefer the *younger* ones, at least ten years my junior. I don't think that makes me a bad person. Please don't think I'm a horrible man. I just figure we only get one good shot at it, might as well go for what you know you want. I mean, I wouldn't want to hurt anyone because they weren't my type and I was just with them to avoid 'being honest' with myself."

He. Did. Not.

I stare blankly at him. I can't fathom his words. I honestly can't. I understand having a type, I also understand not going for someone who doesn't work for you because you don't want to hurt them—like this situation, for example—but this man is being . . . he's just being . . . an asshole.

"Please don't think I'm awful," he says, putting his hands up. "Gosh, I always do this. Put my foot in my mouth. I don't know why. I just figure, you only get one life, you might as well not settle for less than what you want. I'm not attracted to women my own age, I find them unappealing. It wouldn't be fair of me to lead them on, when I know they're not what I want. Nobody should date someone they're not attracted to."

Oh my god. He's making it even worse!

This guy seems to think he's Christian-freaking-Grey.

"And what you want has to be not only young but also attractive. You don't think that's a little . . . well . . . above your limit?"

"You've taken me wrong," he says, but I know I haven't.

I know now why he's single and on a dating site. He's picky, and not only is he picky, he thinks he's *entitled* to be picky. Now, don't get me wrong, I'm sure there are good men out there who don't have the looks but don't let it get to them, and do the right thing. This man, he doesn't have the looks, and yet he still thinks he's entitled to make women the same age as him who aren't as hot as he wants them to be—or as young as he wants them—feel like they're less.

"No," I say, collecting my purse. "I think I've read you just fine. I'm sorry, I think you're too old for me, anyway."

His mouth drops open. "You haven't even given me a chance."

I give him a firm look, making sure I hold his eyes when I speak in a low, snippy tone. "You think you're better than women your own age, and your reasoning is that you prefer younger women, but not only that, they also have to be attractive as well. Why? What makes you think you get such a choice? Let me give you a piece of advice—unless you're

Brad Pitt, you don't get to be so picky. It's shallow, and it's unattractive, and if you want a decent date, perhaps you should try adjusting your ridiculous standards and maybe try being a decent human being."

His mouth opens, then closes.

I don't give him the chance to say anything more. I turn and walk out, not even offering him money for the drink. The dick can pay for it himself. I move quickly out of the restaurant and onto the sidewalk, wave down a cab and climb in, and pulling out my phone the second I've given the driver my address. I text Taylor right away.

> H: You and I are having words. That man was horrible!
>
> T: Oh dear. Was it that bad? Was he at least good-looking?
>
> H: If you call old and balding good-looking . . . then yes.
>
> T: OMG. His profile said he was young, with dark hair, I swear!
>
> H: We're having words about this. Not only was he all those things, he was a shallow jerk, too.
>
> T: I'm sorry. I promise the next one will be better.

I shove my phone back into my purse and huff the entire way home. When the cab arrives at my apartment complex, I pay the driver and climb out, walking through the front doors to the elevator that'll take me to the second floor, where my apartment is. It isn't high up, and I could probably use the stairs, but the elevator is always just right there, and I'm not a fan of stairs. Just as I step in and the doors are about to close, a big hand swings in, stopping them in their tracks.

Detective Ace Henderson steps in.

TWO

If I'm being totally honest with myself, Ace is probably one of the most attractive men I've ever had the pleasure of laying my eyes on. Not that I've seen him a great deal. He's usually heading out as I'm heading in, or the other way around. I've seen him a couple of times in the communal laundry room, but he's always reading and is never up for conversation. There were the few times he left his garbage outside the garbage chute, which totally ticked me off, but outside of that, I don't see him around a good deal. He seems a bit antisocial.

I notice, though, that every time I do see him, he almost always is in a suit, yet he's perpetually scruffy. His hair is always slightly messy, like he's just run his fingers through it, and he has that dark stubble on his jaw.

Don't even get me started on those eyes.

Brown, like liquid chocolate. Framed by the biggest, thickest lashes I've ever seen on a man. They're set into his head perfectly, surrounded by the most incredible masculine features; and then there's that massive body, all the olive skin and those fine, fine muscles. He's the first man I noticed after Ray, even if it was just to enjoy looking at him. I felt guilty at that first flood of lust. It took a while for that guilt to ease.

I swallow.

I've never shared an elevator with him. I've lived here over a year, and we've never ridden up or down together. My eyes slide over to the man as he jabs a thumb at the close button, shutting the doors. It's just us two. There is that incredibly awkward silence going on, where you don't know if you should say anything to break the ice or just pretend the other person isn't in the elevator with you.

"Hi there, neighbor."

Oh. My. God.

Did I just say that?

I just said that.

I might as well slap a sign on my head. A big LOSER sign.

Ace's eyes swing to me. Oh those eyes. So incredibly gorgeous. The kind of eyes that turn your legs to jelly, and your panties into a puddle on the floor. They're intense, and they speak more words than he ever will. Ace stares at me for a long few seconds, then his eyes move back to the door, without even a hello.

Now that's rude.

"I said hello," I mumble. "You could at least say hello back."

Those eyes move to me again. He's massive up close. I swear standing next to his six-foot frame makes me feel two feet tall. Granted, I'm not tall and tend to be on the petite side, but this man makes me feel even smaller than I actually am. He's intimidating, a little scary even. Those bulging muscles, obvious even under the gray suit that fits him so well, don't help. His dark hair is the usual mess, all over the place, like he woke up this morning, got dressed, and walked out of the house without even running a hand through it.

Why am I noticing him so much right now? I mean sure, I've always glanced at him and noticed his looks, but I'm *really* noticing them now. That makes me a little uneasy, and that familiar tinge of guilt squeezes my chest, even though rationally I know there is absolutely no reason for it. There is nothing wrong with noticing other men, or even dating them. I know this.

I do.

"Do I know you?"

His voice is every woman's wet dream: husky, masculine, and deep. I focus on it for only a second, and then his words penetrate. *Do I know you?* Is he serious right now? There is only one other apartment on our floor, which belongs to a little old lady, Lena. How in the hell can he not know who I am? I see him just about every day. I've said hello to him before. He cannot be serious.

"I live right next door to you."

He studies me. "I never noticed you."

He doesn't say that in the kind, oh-I'm-sorry-I-didn't-realize way. No. He says it in the oh-you're-not-noticeable, sorry way. I've said hello so many times, and waved right in his pretty, jerky face. He knows it, too. I'm sure of it. Nobody is that stupid. So he's chosen to be a pig about it, for no good reason. My spine straightens and anger bubbles in my chest. I've had just about enough of the male population tonight. First Greg and his shallow personality, and now Ace.

No.

Just no.

"I don't know what cereal box you got your manners manual out of, buddy," I snap. "But you're incredibly rude."

One dark brow shoots up, just as the elevator dings and the door opens. I storm out first, horrified at the audacity of the man. I take the four steps to the left from the elevator to my door, and pull out my keys. Glancing over at Ace as he stands by his door a few feet down, watching me.

"That's right, I live right here. I'm the woman who says hello to you, who you so rudely ignore—and then insult. And no," I mutter, shoving my key in the lock, "I will never be lending you milk."

I kick the door open, and then pop my head back out. "Or sugar!"

I slam the door. The first thing I do is call Taylor. I'm furious and she needs to know exactly what I think.

"Still upset?" she answers, her tone light.

"I'm not going on another date, Taylor. Absolutely not. I thought you should know that."

"Aw, come on, I'm sorry. I didn't know he was a liar. It's a blink date website, I can only filter it down to basics: age, height, hair color, things like that. It's meant to be a surprise, so I don't get to see photos. That's what makes it a mystery . . . and fun. Some people are liars, I guess, and categorize themselves wrong. But—"

"Exactly. There are probably a thousand other liars out there. No. No more."

"You promised me three, please, Hart."

I huff, close my eyes for calm. Men. Maybe I'm better off without them.

"I don't think I can handle another one like that," I mutter, rubbing my temple with my pointer finger.

"Well, let's hope the next ones aren't liars. I'm sure it'll be fine. Worst case, they're not and you have to cope with a few lousy dates. At least you're getting out there."

I exhale. I promised three. I'll give her three.

"Fine, but honestly, I don't have a good deal of patience left."

She giggles lightly. "Take a deep breath. It isn't so bad. Besides aren't these great stories to have?"

I growl.

She laughs.

"Good night, Taylor. I love you even though I hate you right now."

"Love you too!"

This night sucks.

THREE

"I cannot believe I'm doing this again," I mumble to myself as I walk down the sidewalk towards another bar, where I'm meeting yet another man.

I swear, if this one is awful, Taylor is never meddling in my love life again. There will *not* be a date number three. There is only so much a girl can put up with before shit starts getting old. I draw my creeper line at two. So this one had better be damned good, or that's it.

I stop at the outside entrance to the bar, where I'm supposed to be meeting this guy, and wait. I glance around, my eyes scanning the groups of people hovering around. It's a nice place, with modern décor and tables scattered under some big umbrellas outside. I run my hands down the black dress I'm wearing. It's a V-neck, tighter at the top but loose and flowing from the waist down. Sexy, but not inviting. I pinned my hair up with a few gold clips, and put a light dusting of makeup on.

I have a feeling I may be overdressed for the

occasion, judging by the jeans and cute tops most of the other women sitting around are wearing. This just makes me feel even more nervous inside, and because of that, I don't pay much attention to the throat clearing behind me. Only when I feel a tap on my shoulder do I spin around.

I'm faced with an extremely good-looking man, holding a rose. That's the first thing I notice. He has sandy brown hair long enough to fall over his forehead, blue eyes, and a tall but lean build. He's dressed nicely, but casually, in a blink date website gray tee and a pair of dark denim jeans. His eyes scan over me, and he flashes a genuine smile that really lights up his face. He's handsome, without a doubt.

"Are you Hartley?"

"Yes." I smile.

He beams, his smile getting bigger. He has dimples. Cute. He extends a hand and I take it, as he curls his warm, soft fingers around mine. "I'm Richard. It's wonderful to meet you. You look lovely tonight."

My nerves ease. Okay, so this one seems nice. He's nice-looking, too. That's two off the checklist. Maybe we'll be able to have a decent conversation and I'll lose the urge to murder Taylor. I let my shoulders relax and give him my best smile. "Thank you, would you like to go inside?"

"Yes, I would," he says.

I take the rose, impressed by the sweet gesture. I give him a genuine thank-you, and we both turn and enter the bar. It's modern inside too, decked out in black and red, giving it a sleek, easygoing appeal. Richard leads me to a big red booth and I slide in. He sits across from me, placing his elbows on the table and focusing on me. A waitress comes over right away, and looks down at us. "Hi there, can I get you both a drink?"

"Just a rum and coke for me," Richard says to her and then glances over to me.

I order a vodka and lime, and then focus back on the man sitting across from me when the waitress disappears. I don't really know where to start the conversation, so I go with the usual questions.

"What do you do for a living, Richard?"

"I'm a lawyer," he tells me. "It's a very demanding job, but I do enjoy it. What about you?"

A lawyer. Very impressive.

"At the moment, I'm studying to become a midwife, so I'm just working until I'm finished with that."

His brows go up. "A midwife. What made you want to do that?"

I shrug. "I started as a nurse, but would love to work in the field with babies, so I decided to take it to the next level."

He nods, impressed. "Admirable."

"Yeah." I smile. "It's a lot of hours, but I think it'll be worth it."

He nods thoughtfully. "My ex-girlfriend was a nurse. It took its toll on her, too. But it'll be a very rewarding career. I think it always is when you're able to help other people."

I nod in agreement, crossing my ankles under the table. "Yes, it is tiring though."

The waitress returns with our drinks, placing them down, and I take a sip of mine.

Richard continues talking. "Yes, she used to come home exhausted. Poor girl. I always felt so sorry for her."

Ah, okay. It's a little weird to bring up the ex-girlfriend in the first few minutes of the conversation with a girl you're on a date with, but maybe he's just anxious and can't think of anything else to talk about. Or maybe he's one of those men who just don't really have any setbacks when it comes to talking about exes, because it's in the past.

"Yes, it's demanding work." I decide to continue.

"Indeed it is." He nods. "This one time, she worked over twenty-four hours. I didn't see her. She never stopped, you know?"

Okay, enter more awkward ex-girlfriend talk. Maybe I should change the subject?

"Do you enjoy your job?" I ask. "It must be tiring as well. I hear lawyers work some long hours."

He nods. "Yes. Mandy, my ex, she didn't like it. She said she hated that I got called out all the time, but it's a demanding job. I work more than I enjoy life sometimes. And she just couldn't seem to understand that, you know?"

Oh dear.

He's hung up on his ex.

Sigh. Might as well scrap this one as a potential person to date and just go with the flow. I have nothing else to do tonight, and I dressed up. Besides, I love a good story. So I settle in, sip my drink, and go for it.

"What happened with Mandy?"

His eyes sadden. Here we go. I'm going to need a double shot. I can already tell by his expression that whatever she did to him, really hurt.

"She cheated on me. It broke my heart. To be honest, I'm still recovering. I thought dating would help."

Poor guy, that's the absolute worst. I can handle a lot of things in a relationship, but cheating . . . I don't think I could live with that. It's awful.

"I'm really sorry. That must have been awful. I agree dating might help, but probably not until you're ready."

"I don't know if I am, you know?" he agrees. "I loved her. I wanted a future with her, I just feel like I'll never love anyone again . . ."

For the next three solid hours, I comfort Richard over his breakup with Mandy, who sounds like an absolute bitch. During this time, I nod, give him advice, and even pat him on the shoulder every so often. He's a good sport, thanking me over and over and apologizing for leading me on. He even pays for all the drinks. I can't deny that, as horrible as the story was, it was nice to talk about someone else's problems and not focus on my own.

It also makes me realize there are so many people out there struggling, and I don't want to always be seen as one of them. I lost my husband, and it still hurts daily, but I also have a chance to make something of my life. Seeing Richard, and seeing his pain, only makes it clear that I can't reflect that on other people for the rest of my days. I have to move on eventually, and I want to, for the first time in what seems like forever, I actually want to consider what it might be like to live again.

Maybe Taylor was right, maybe these dates are good for me, even if I don't actually walk away with a partner out of it. Maybe they're just a good way for me to see that I've been living in a shell for four years, and I need to find myself and get back out there. I know Raymond would kick me right up the backside if he knew I was still holding onto him and not making something of my life. He would want this for me—that much I'm sure of with a hundred percent certainty.

For the first time in a long time, I don't feel the crushing guilt at the thought of moving on.

Yes, maybe Taylor was right. Brat.

Once Richard has gone, I get a cab back home. I call Taylor the second I get in the car. I'm not unhappy about my evening, but this woman seriously needs to start paying more attention to the men she's picking for me. I can only imagine what she's going to present me with next.

"So?" she answers on the first ring, her voice all chipper and excited. "You were gone for a while, can I assume it went well?"

I snort. "You would be assuming wrong. The man was hung up on his ex-girlfriend, and I spent three hours comforting him. But outside of that, he wasn't a bad guy and it was entertaining, but no more dates like this one—please."

"Comforting him? Seriously? That's a little funny."

"Yes, seriously. I honestly felt sorry for the poor guy by the end of it."

"You at least made a friend out of him, right?"

"I'm not going on another blind date if they're all going to be like this," I say to get my point across once more. "As fun as it is to get out, and as much as I don't want to admit you were right in pushing me, there is only so much I can handle doing it this way."

She exhales, long and dramatic. "Give me one more. I promise you he'll be good, I'll make sure of it."

I make a dissatisfied *hmmm* sound in my throat.

"I don't believe you, considering the other two were meant to be good, and turned out not to be. I'm starting to think you're finding this more entertaining than I am."

She laughs again. "I know, I'm sorry. Please, one more. I promise it won't be awful."

I exhale with a groan. "One more, but I swear, I *swear* . . . if this one is bad, I'm setting you up on three dates myself so you can endure this too."

"Deal."

I mumble a curse under my breath. "I'm about to enter my building, I'll call you later. Make the last one good, Tay."

"On it."

I hang up and step through the front doors and straight into a hard, muscled chest. I bounce off it, as if I weigh no more than a sack of feathers. I stumble backwards, tripping and landing on my butt with a humph. My dress rides up, and I quickly squirm, trying to shuffle it down before the entire foyer sees my underwear.

I look up to see Ace, staring down at me. His hand is already extending towards my arm, no doubt to pull me up, but I wave it off, horrified that he probably just got a good view of my underwear. At least I can be assured it was good underwear. Black lace. But there is also the fact that I just fell on my ass in front of him. Highly unattractive. Not that I care what he thinks.

"I didn't see you there," he murmurs. "Sorry."

I scramble awkwardly a few times, and then push to my feet, with only a slight amount of grunting, and dust my bottom off before looking at him. "Of course you didn't. Whatever. It's fine."

I try to step past him, but he stops me with that husky, damned amazing voice. It sends shivers up my spine, which I try very hard to ignore.

"Don't forget this."

He holds out my cell phone. I glance at it. Whoops. I must have dropped it, and I was about to storm off. I take the phone from his hand, and my fingers graze his as I do. Calloused. Rough. Hot.

"Thanks," I mumble to my feet.

I'm not giving him any more than that after his comment the other night. Nope. I will not. Even if he did just save my cell phone's life. I shove the phone right down the front of my dress, and stare at him. For a few long seconds, we just stare at each other, neither of us breaking eye contact. Something flares inside me as we lock eyes. Determination. Stubbornness. Feelings that have long lay dormant. They terrify, confuse, and excite me all at the same time.

His brow quirks, but he doesn't say anything. Instead he finally breaks eye contact and nods his head, disappearing out the doors I just came in through. I turn and watch him go, my eyes dropping to long, thick legs that stride with ease. Yes, he definitely stirs something in me. I just can't put my finger on what.

It's probably best if it stays that way, too.

FOUR

"This one is good, I promise," Taylor tells me on the phone as I rush to the elevator, already late for date number three. "I even messaged him myself, to make sure he wasn't telling lies about his profile. He seems like a good honest man, well spoken. I think you'll thank me for this one."

Panting, I say back, "He better be, Taylor. Honestly, I'm not going to be happy if I have to endure yet another dud."

She giggles as I step into the elevator, still with my back to the door.

"I mean honestly, I know I've been alone for four years, but there is a limit to what I'm willing to put up with. As much as helping a broken man made me feel good about myself, it wasn't what I'd call a good date. So I hope we're lucky with number three."

I turn around to check that the door is shut, then squeal when I see Ace standing there, staring at me. In the elevator. I didn't hear him come in. I never see him riding on the elevator, and now suddenly he's always here. Just my luck. My cheeks instantly turn red, and I fumble an "I'll call you later" to Taylor before disconnecting, horrified that Ace probably heard my entire conversation. Now he knows I go on blind dates, and I have no doubt that whatever is going through his mind right now is something along the lines of "pathetic."

Not making eye contact, I step over and press the button to take us to the lobby. Then I stand by the wall and cross my arms, still keeping my eyes to the ground. I don't know if Ace expects me to talk with him, but if he thinks I'm going to, he's sadly mistaken.

"Blind date, huh?"

So he did hear what I was saying. And of all the times he chooses to make conversation first, it's about my lame love life and the fact that I am allowing my best friend to set me up on blind dates.

I shoot him a scowl, mostly to hide my utter embarrassment, and I mutter, "It's rude to listen to other people's conversations, but what should I expect, you're hardly polite."

His brows go up, and then he gets that broody look right back on his too perfect face. "Pretty hard not to hear you when you're basically yelling it to the entire hall."

I scoff. "I was not yelling it, and there is only one other person on this floor. So I think that counts as eavesdropping. Which, I repeat, is rude."

"You're not a very nice lady, are you?"

My mouth drops open. "I beg your pardon." I lift a hand and wiggle a finger in his face. "I have said hello to you, on numerous occasions—I even waved once—and you, mister, were the one who ignored it. Not only that, when you did speak to me, you had no freaking idea who I was. So, it's not me that isn't nice, that's all on you."

He crosses his big arms over his chest, stretching that suit tight. I try, very hard, to keep my eyes on his when all they want to do is scour slowly down his body to get yet another mental image to torment my mind with. I know how good that suit looks, pulled across his muscles.

"You're mouthy for someone so small."

He. Did. Not.

I snap out of my thoughts and my mouth drops open, then closes. And then I growl, "And you're arrogant for someone so, big . . ."

Jesus. *Big.*

I want to slap myself.

The elevator dings, and the doors slide open. I go charging out, horrified and angry at Ace and his rude behavior. I won't take it. I'm already in a bad enough mood as it is, after spending an entire night up studying, before working a full day at the café down the road, where I waitress. Now I'm about to endure date number three, which I'm less than happy about but want to get out of the way so Taylor can finally leave me alone.

"Don't trip on your way out," Ace mutters. I stop dead in my tracks and turn around.

A frustrated sound escapes my throat and I throw my hands up. "Seriously, if I was bigger . . . I'd . . . I'd . . . smack you!"

With that, I storm out the front doors as my Uber pulls up. I don't stop and see if Ace exits the building too, I get in and then cross my arms, brooding the entire way to the restaurant. The driver has the radio blaring in the car, and I zone in on the story about the recent murders that have been happening. I remember hearing people at the café talking about it.

"This evening, another body was found. The third murder like this in the past year. While that doesn't seem like a high number, the police are investigating if it's the work of a serial killer, due to the familiar pattern with each victim. So far we can only confirm that they have all been killed in the same way and left to hang with a bowtie around their necks. At this stage, the name and age of the most recent victim is still unknown."

I shiver.

That's the third murder in this area, now. I had heard about the first one. It sent half the city into a frenzy, but police put it down to a sicko who decided to have a random kill. But then it happened again, and people got even more stressed out, when it was made known that the kill was identical to the first. Now a third. I rub my arms, suddenly feeling cold.

What is this world coming to?

"Terrible, isn't it?" The driver says, glancing at me in the rearview mirror.

"Yeah," I agree. "It is. I hope they find him soon."

"Me too. Three young lives ended in a horrific way. I hope they catch the bastard and give him what he deserves."

This person—whoever it is—is twisted. I don't know much about the killings, but from what I've seen on the news, he torments his victims, making them seem crazy by doing things to make them think they're losing their minds, and then he takes them.

I don't know how he takes them, or how he lures them away, but he kills them, and when he's done, he hangs them in a tree, with a bowtie around their neck. I saw an article recently saying the police think he's been planning these murders for some time, and that they believe he has more lined up, due to how frequently he is taking his victims.

This girl, the one they have just found, I wonder how long he tormented her for? Did her family even know she was missing? Did anyone suspect something was wrong? Does she even have a family, or does he pick the ones who are alone? I don't know, but the possibilities are terrifying. I can only imagine what she went through. God, I don't even want to think about it too long, it sends shivers down my spine.

I send a mental reminder to myself to check my locks when I get home, just to be sure.

When we arrive at the restaurant, I climb out of the car. I glance around—it's a really nice place, a small Italian restaurant with warm lighting and big booths both inside and out. I let my eyes scan the people, seeing if there is anyone waiting, but it doesn't seem there are any single men standing around, so I make my way over to a free table and sit down, glancing at my phone. I'm a little late. Maybe the guy won't show and I can go home.

"You must be Hartley."

The smooth, masculine voice has my head jerking up. My eyes widen when I see a good-looking man standing by the table, dressed in a pair of dark pants, a suede jacket, and a black tee. He's exceptionally good-looking, with flawless pale skin, soft blue eyes, and mousy brown hair that's trimmed neatly and brushed off to the side. He's got the features of a model, not at all rugged, but perfectly proportioned to be on the cover of a magazine. He's tall, too. Lovely.

"Hi," I say, my voice coming out far huskier than I would have anticipated, but he's definitely caught me off guard, I can't deny that. "Yes, I am."

His eyes light up, and he smiles, making him that much more good-looking. "Pleasure to meet you. I'm Jacob."

Jacob.

Hot name.

I smile back, and this time it's a real smile, not a forced one. "It's wonderful to meet you, Jacob."

So far, so good.

He nods to the chair beside me. "Mind if I take a seat?"

"Of course," I say, waving a hand at the chair.

Jacob sits down, smiling at me from across the table. Yep, he's certainly easy on the eyes. He's also picked a really classy restaurant. Incredible food. I've been here a few times before, it's most certainly memorable.

"Would you like a drink?" he offers.

Sweet Jesus. Yes.

"Yes, please."

He waves down a young waiter, who strolls over, smiling at the both of us. "Hi there, what can I get you?"

Jacob looks to me. "What would you like?"

"Just a vodka and lime, please."

"And I'll have a whiskey, neat," he orders.

Double hot.

"Coming right up."

When the waiter has gone, Jacob looks to me. "I'm sorry if I'm not doing very well at this. It's the first time I've dated in a long time, I'm afraid."

I exhale a little, fully relaxing into my chair. Maybe this wasn't such a bad idea after all. "Me too, so if I screw up, forgive me."

His eyes warm and his lips twitch. "I can't imagine you'd screw up. You're far too beautiful for that."

I flush. "Thank you."

He flashes me that all-American boy-next-door smile again. "What do you do for a living, Hartley?"

"Call me Hart, please, and I'm studying to be a midwife. I work as a waitress in between."

His brows go up. "That's very impressive!"

I flush. "Thank you. What about you? What do you do?"

"I'm an interior designer."

My brows go up now too. "Wow, that's inspiring. Does that keep you busy?"

"Extremely," he smiles. "I currently have four jobs this week, and another three booked for next."

The waiter returns with our drinks, and we both take sips before continuing. "How does that work?" I ask, curious. "Do they ask for your opinion and you design them something?"

He nods. "Sometimes, yes. I basically go in, speak with them, look at their house and the style and design, and then I create a plan on a program that I have on my computer. I show it to them, and then we adjust it to suit their needs."

"Wow, that's amazing. You must have a creative mind, to be able to come up with something like that. I've seen the work of some interior designers—it's incredible."

He looks flattered by my compliment and gives me a small, almost shy smile. "Yeah, I do have somewhat of a creative mind."

Finally, a conversation that seems to be flowing well and a man who seems normal.

"Have you lived in Denver long?" Jacob asks, sipping his drink, scanning me with those great-looking blue eyes.

"All my life. I used to live just on the outskirts with my husband for ten years, but sadly he passed four years ago."

Jacob's eyes soften, and in a kind voice, he says, "I'm terribly sorry, that must have been awful. Can I ask what happened?"

"He was in a car accident," I tell him.

"Again, I'm sorry. That would have been hard to deal with. Is that why you moved closer to town?"

I nod. "Yes, plus it was closer to the hospital where I do a good deal of my training and assessments. So it made more sense to be closer to the city."

He nods thoughtfully. "Do you enjoy living close to the city?"

"Yes and no," I admit. "Sometimes I find that I miss the quiet of living out of town, but I do enjoy the convenience."

He nods in agreement. "And do you have any family close by?"

I shake my head. "No, my mother passed away before I lost my husband. My father is still alive, but is traveling overseas. I don't have any siblings."

Jacob nods. "I'm sorry to hear about your mother, but it seems like your father is doing well for himself."

I smile. "Yeah, he's happy. Good for him, too. I'm glad he's out there getting the most out of his life. It's so short, you know?"

"I absolutely agree," he murmurs, sipping his drink again.

"What about you?" I ask. "Do you have any family?"

He shakes his head. "No, I lost my parents when I was younger. A tragic accident took them from me."

My heart breaks for him. I know how losing someone unexpectedly feels. "I'm so sorry, that's terrible."

He shrugs. "On to more appealing subjects," he laughs. "What do you like to do for fun? Any hobbies?"

That was a rapid change of subject. Now I'm curious about his parents, but I don't say anything more because I don't want to pry. And, from personal experience, I know what it's like when people push you to answer questions about the loss of a loved one and you just don't want to talk about it. So, I let it go.

"I wish I could say I had some crazy talent." I roll my eyes. "But sadly, I'm just a plain Jane. I do love to read, though. I guess you could call that a hobby."

"Certainly, and you're more than a plain Jane." He grins. "And I'm the same. I don't have any hobbies, either."

I laugh softly. "I guess we can be simple together."

He chuckles. "I guess so."

I spend the next three hours talking easily with Jacob. We have dinner and then he offers to drive me home. When we arrive at my apartment building, he's a proper gentleman and keeps his distance, staying at the door and not asking to come inside, even though I'm sure he probably wants to. Part of me wants him to, even just for coffee, but I know that wouldn't be right, for either of us.

I don't really know him, and we had a great night. I think it's best to leave it at that.

"Thank you for a wonderful night," I say to him, leaning against the post just outside the front doors.

"You're welcome. I had a great time. I'd love to see you again, if you'd like?"

I study him. Yes, I think I would like to get to know him better. He's easygoing, handsome, and we had some good laughs. Even if it doesn't progress further, I feel like even a friendship with this man would be worthwhile. Tonight is the first time in a long time I've enjoyed myself. I didn't realize how much I was holding myself back until right now.

"I would like that." I beam. "I'll give you my phone number."

I give him my phone number while he dials. He calls my phone, so I have his, and then tucks his phone back into his pocket. "I'll give you a call in the morning," he says, giving me a warm, friendly expression. "Thanks again, it was a great night."

I nod, in full agreement. "Yes it was. Good night, Jacob."

"Good night, Hartley."

I walk through the front doors with a huge smile on my face.

Maybe Taylor was right.

Maybe this was a good idea after all.

FIVE

"You look beautiful, Hartley," Jacob says, taking my hand and pulling me towards the movie theater.

We're on our second "official" date. So far, things with Jacob are going really well. He's kind, and funny, and he's really easy to talk to. I find myself at ease with him, never feeling awkward or uncomfortable. Conversation flows naturally between us, and if there is ever a pause, Jacob quickly fills it with questions about my life. He listens when I speak, seemingly really taking in everything I'm saying.

That's a nice feeling. Comforting.

Tonight he suggested a movie, and then dinner afterwards. I honestly can't remember the last time I went to a movie. It was a long time ago, with Raymond, possibly at the beginning of our relationship. There is something strangely romantic about going to a movie with someone you like, feeling their hand brush yours, or their shoulder, as you sit close together.

"Thank you," I smile at Jacob, taking in his clean cut look. "You look great, too."

He's wearing a pair of jeans, dark denim—they look new they're in such good condition. Paired with the jeans, is a black button-down shirt that he has rolled at the sleeves. He's got his brown hair brushed back neatly, and overall, looks incredible. I smooth my hands down my navy blue dress. It's tighter at the top, but flares out at the bottom and rests right around my knees. I left my hair down for the occasion, and opted for just a little mascara.

As we approach, there is a group of teens sitting just outside the doors, laughing a little too loud. I'd bet anything they snuck alcohol into whatever movie they just came out of. As we walk past, one of them stands and walks towards me. As she goes past, her shoulder bumps against mine, rocking me a bit. She's a bigger girl, with cropped red hair.

"Watch where you're going!" she snaps at me. "Bitch."

We stop walking, and Jacob's body goes tight. He turns slowly and stares at the girl, who is glaring at me, almost looking like she wants me to give her a reaction.

"Mind your manners," Jacob says to her, his voice firm but not angry.

"I beg your pardon?" The teen throws back, putting a hand on her hip and getting the attention of the other teens who all look our way.

"I said," Jacob says back calmly, "mind your manners. We're here for a movie. We're not bothering you. If you want to start something with someone, go and find another person. Do not speak to my lady like that."

My heart flutters. He's sticking up for me. It doesn't matter who, what, where, when or why, if someone sticks up for you, and is willing to defend you, it feels damned wonderful. I think I fall for him just a bit more.

"What are you going to do about it?" the girl throws back.

Jacob stares at her, and there must be something in his eyes because she drops her hand from her hip. "I'm not going to do anything except take my girl inside and watch a movie with her. I'm simply telling you to mind your manners, it'll do you good in the future."

With that, he turns us and we walk into the theater. I look over at him with a huge smile on my face.

"What are you smiling at?" he asks, raising his brows.

"You defended me."

He looks confused. "Of course I did. Nobody should speak to you like that."

"I know, but . . . it just felt nice. Thank you."

He leans in, brushing his lips across my forehead. "I'll always defend a woman, Hartley. It's the right thing to do."

Swoon.

"Now," he says, stepping back and clapping his hands together. "Are we doing action or romance?"

"I get to pick?" I tease.

He laughs. "You most certainly do. But only for this date, after that it's my turn."

He winks at me and I giggle. "Let's do action."

He raises his brows. "I like a girl who knows no boundaries."

I smile. "What can I say? I like to live danger-
ously!"

"Indeed," he murmurs. "Action it is."

He buys our tickets, some popcorn and drinks,
and finds a seat in the back row. Jacob hands me the
popcorn and for a few moments, we just sit there
in silence, snacking, and then he turns to me and
says in a low voice, so as not to disturb anyone,
"Look at that couple down in front."

I look to where he points and see a couple practically chewing each other's faces off, hands everywhere, limbs tangled. They're young, maybe in their
late teens.

"Oh to be that young again," I laugh softly.

"The movie hasn't even started yet," Jacob
chuckles.

"Looks like we're in for an entertaining evening
then."

Jacob laughs, reaching over and taking my hand,
making my heart flutter. "Looks like it."

This is nice. Sweet. Comforting.

Yes.

Just what I need.

"Lena, hi," I smile to my elderly neighbor as Jacob
and I make our way towards my apartment later
that night after we've gorged ourselves on pizza. I
was already full after eating all the popcorn at the
movie, but the moment I smelled the pizza, I had to
have some.

I'm certain Jacob could roll me into my apartment if I let him.

"Hello, dear," Lena smiles, walking towards us.
She was just about to enter her apartment, but

stopped when I called out to her. She's got to be in her late seventies, but she holds her own well. I always see her carrying her laundry or dragging her garbage out. Every time I offer to help her, she waves and does it herself. She's stubborn, and she's proud, and she's one of the nicest old ladies I've met.

"Lena, this is Jacob."

Jacob steps forward and extends a hand. "Wonderful to meet you. Hartley told me you make some pretty incredible cookies. I'd love to try them sometime."

Lena flushes. "Oh, oh, that's kind of her. I'll drop some over next time I bake a batch, and she can share them with you."

"That sounds wonderful."

Lena looks to me. "How have you been, dear?"

"Very well, thank you."

"I saw Taylor earlier, she was looking for you. I'm not sure if she's still waiting or not. I told her I thought you might be out."

Taylor has a spare key to my apartment. I wonder if she's still waiting there? It'd be great to introduce her to Jacob, I'd like her to meet him.

"Thank you, I'll go and see if she's still there."

"It was lovely to meet you Jacob, and Hartley, I'll see you soon."

"Bye, Lena." I wave.

When she's gone, Jacob and I continue down the hall. "She's nice. Have you known her long?"

"Just since I've lived here. She checks on me often, even though it should be the other way around. She's really kind, I like her a lot."

"She is."

We reach my apartment, which is just down the hall from Lena's, and I unlock the door, going inside. As predicted, Taylor is sitting on the kitchen bench and her pretty blonde head swivels around when she hears us. Her eyes widen when she sees Jacob and she leaps out of her seat quickly. "Oh my god. I forgot you were on a date. I thought you might have just been out, so I waited. Oh gosh. I'm sorry."

I laugh. "It's okay. Jacob, I'd like you to meet my slightly crazy, slightly deranged best friend Taylor."

Taylor's cheeks flush, but she keeps that award-winning smile as she walks over and extends her hand to Jacob. "Hi, Jacob. You have me to thank for meeting this wonderful catch of a woman."

Jacob laughs, shaking her hand. "Is that so?"

I flush. "Well, Taylor may have had a hand in pushing me back into the dating world."

"Well, I'm glad she did and I was lucky enough to get picked," Jacob says, winking at me.

"I like him already," Taylor beams. "I won't hold you two up, I'm sure you'd like some time alone."

"Certainly not," Jacob says. "Please stay. I'll make some coffee if you guide me to where you keep everything."

"Yes, stay." I smile to my friend, thrilled that Jacob doesn't mind hanging out with my best friend.

"Okay then," Taylor says, giving me a thumbs-up when Jacob moves into the kitchen. "Swoon," she whispers.

I look over at Jacob with a smile. "I know! He's nice, isn't he?"

"He is. And good-looking too!"

"Yeah, I like him."

She pretends to give herself a pat on the back. "I knew I'd pick one good one. I'm happy for you, Hart. You look . . . carefree tonight. For the first time in a long time, and that makes me happy."

I smile at my best friend. I might have been against her setting me up on blind dates, but I have to admit she's right. I like Jacob, and I'd like to see where it goes, but more than that, I really like living a life outside of my job and my apartment. It's been so long since I've let my hair down and gone out to have some fun. I needed it more than I thought I did.

"Yeah, thank you. I didn't realize I needed it until I started doing it," I admit.

"I'm glad, really I am." She reaches over and squeezes my arm. "You deserve it."

She's right.

Maybe I do.

SIX

"So, it's still going well between you and Jacob?" Taylor asks, strolling past my kitchen with a bag of muffins in her hands.

There is a little bakery just down the street that makes the most amazing muffins. Taylor regularly stops by before work and will grab us a few along with their great coffee.

"Yeah." I smile. "He's really nice. We've been out four times now, but we talk every day. I think it's going somewhere."

Taylor places the bag down, and then claps her hands. "I knew it, I knew he was a good one. I really liked him. Say thank you to your bestie. If it wasn't for me you'd still be sewing buttons on blouses."

"Excuse me," I say, wiggling a finger in her face. "But that is my favorite blouse."

She rolls her eyes. "Yeah yeah, that's what they all say. So, tell me more—has he kissed you yet?"

"A few times," I say, beaming.

"But you haven't . . . you know?" she questions.

"No," I say quickly. "Gosh, I'm not in a hurry to go to that level. I really want to take this slow. I'm in no rush. I'm just enjoying it as it comes, without all the complications of moving it to the next level too quickly. It's nice right now. Carefree and easy-going."

"Oh I agree, and he really seems like a keeper. Did you ever hear back from any of the others?"

I frown. "Greg sent me a message once on social media—he must have looked me up—apologizing for the date. I never answered."

Taylor scrunches up her nose. "He *should* apologize."

A knock at my door distracts me from the conversation. I give Taylor a look, wondering who it might be, but she shrugs. I walk over, undoing the chain and pulling the door open to see Ace standing in my doorway, looking broody, and maybe a little sheepish. For a moment, I just stare at him with wide eyes. I have no idea why he's here, but I'm shocked, shocked enough to have no words until he holds up a small jug.

"I need to borrow some milk."

I blink.

Did he just say he needs to borrow . . . milk?

"You're kidding me, right?" I say, snapping out of my trance. "Is this some sort of joke?"

He looks at me like I have something wrong with me, and mutters, "No. I have guests, and I ran out of milk. Lena doesn't have any. That left you."

Oh. So he knows Lena's name, but never thought to come and get mine. Rude. Double rude.

I cock a brow, and throw a hand on my hip. "Introduced yourself to our other neighbor, did you?"

He looks up to the ceiling, as if trying to gather himself. I take the chance to look him over. Casual blue jeans, a tight-fitting gray tee, no shoes. Damn. Hot. "She brings me"—he clears his throat, looking back to me—"cookies."

I snort. Lena is kind like that. Every time she bakes, she brings me something, I guess she brings him some, too.

Smothering a laugh, I say, "Well, it wouldn't have killed you to come and say hello to me, or hell, just a nod would have been nice."

He makes a grumbling sound, and wiggles the milk jug a little, as if trying to bring my attention to it. "Still going on about that?"

Hmmm. He's right. I really need to let it go.

I cross my arms. "I told you I wasn't going to lend you milk, or sugar . . ."

The muscle in his jaw jumps. "Well, I'm askin' you to borrow some. Are you going to give it to me, or do I have to go back and tell my mom, who drove twelve hours to see me, that my neighbor didn't want to lend me milk because I didn't say hello to her?"

Smart-ass.

Damn him. I can't deny his poor mother, even if I want to throttle him.

"I'm sure your mother would be appalled by your lack of manners. I'm very certain if I told her how rude you are, she'd probably give you a stern talking to."

He grunts. "Are you this annoying to everyone you meet, or am I just lucky enough to get all of it?"

I raise my brows. "Do you want that milk or not?"

There goes that jaw muscle again. "You know how far the store is from here, so that would be a yes. I didn't come here to chat."

"That's obvious," I mutter. "You could, at the very least, say please."

He inhales through his nose, and then bites out a "Please."

"There now," I say, snatching the jug out of his hand. "That wasn't so hard."

I turn and strut into my apartment, feeling pretty good about my little remark. Taylor wiggles her brows as I go past, a cheeky grin on her face. "That was kind of funny. I didn't know you two even spoke."

I shrug. "We don't. I've just called him rude, on more than one occasion."

"You didn't share this with me!" she whisper-yells.

"Soon," I whisper-yell back. "He needs milk."

I get him his milk, and then close the fridge, walking back to the door where he's still standing, staring through the space and into my apartment. I thrust the jug at him and look at him expectantly when he takes it from my hands. "You should really get your locks changed, they're terrible. And that back window is flimsy. An old woman could break into it. You might want to look into that."

With that, he turns and strides off down the hall.

"You're welcome!" I call out after him.

I could swear he raises his hand and wiggles his fingers just slightly, but I'm probably imagining things. The man doesn't have manners. I close the door and turn back to Taylor, who is pretty much standing on top of me, peering over my shoulder where Ace just disappeared to.

"That man is so damn fine. Have you taken a look at his ass?"

I turn around and shoot her a look.

"What?" she says innocently, batting her eyelashes. "I'm just saying."

"I have not looked at his ass. I'm too busy studying his rude, jerky face."

I lied. I have totally looked at his ass.

More than once.

"You're a terrible liar," she laughs. "Now come and tell me more about Jacob. I want to know all the juicy details."

We sit on the sofa, and I spend the next few hours telling her about Jacob.

And *all* the juicy details.

I stare at the item of clothing, holding it in my hand for a long, long moment. So long I could swear my fingers go numb. I just look down at it. It's so familiar. I should know because *he* used to wear it every Sunday when we'd watch football together. It was his favorite. We brought it when we went on a vacation to Thailand. The old, gray T-shirt is more than familiar to me.

What I don't understand is why it's sitting on my kitchen table.

It's early morning, just past eight, and I woke to find the shirt just draped over the table, like it had been placed there. Raymond's items have been boxed up since about six months after he passed, sitting in my spare room until I can bring myself to either put them in storage or finally part with them. I taped those boxes closed. I'm sure I did.

Shaking my head, I walk down the hall, the shirt still gripped tightly in my fingers, and I push open the door to my spare room. I walk over to the box labeled CLOTHING and I study it. Sealed shut. It doesn't even look like it has been tampered with. Maybe I didn't pack this shirt? I rack my brain trying to remember if I put it in, but I don't remember. It was an emotional day packing away all his belongings, I don't recall any particular moments like that.

Maybe I didn't pack it, but that doesn't explain how it got onto the kitchen table.

Maybe I was sleepwalking? I've been known to do that in my time, but never to the extreme of picking up items of clothing and putting them on a table. Though it was what was meant to be our wedding anniversary two days ago, and my emotions were a little all over the place, so maybe subconsciously I did somehow manage to get to the shirt and put it on the table.

It's the only explanation I can conjure up right now.

Nothing else has been touched.

I'm overthinking this.

I clutch the shirt and take it into my room, placing it on my desk folded neatly, then I go out and get ready for my shift. The shirt lingers in the back of my mind, consuming my thoughts so much I don't hear the knocking until it becomes a little louder and I snap out of my trance. Rushing over to the door, I swing it open to find Jacob standing there, two coffees in his hand.

"Sorry, I hope I didn't wake you." He smiles. "Good morning."

I glance down at the coffee, then at him, and say in a soft tone, "Morning. Come in."

He studies me, his eyes narrowing. "Are you okay, sweetheart?"

He's taken to calling me sweetheart in the last few days, and I will admit, it is kind of nice. It's been a long time since anyone has spoken to me with such affection. Raymond was an affectionate man, one of the very few I've met who wasn't afraid to show a woman how he felt. It was a quality I loved about him. Something that made living with him a peaceful, fun, happy experience.

"Ah, yeah, I guess."

I'm still distracted. Why would I find a shirt when sleeping and put it on the table? I just don't understand where I would've even found it. I just can't seem to wrap my mind around it, even though I'm sure the explanation is a simple one.

"You don't look okay," Jacob says, and I focus on him again. "Tell me what's happened?"

Should I tell him? Will he think I'm crazy? Gosh. What if he does? No. He wouldn't. He's a nice guy, one of the best. He'll probably be able to set me straight, help me see it a little more clearly.

"It's just, well this might sound a little nuts . . ."

He hands me my coffee and I take it gratefully, moving out of the way as he steps inside. "I don't think it'll sound nuts. Talk to me."

I close the door and exhale. "I found one of my husband's shirts on the kitchen table this morning, but the thing is, I'm sure I packed it away in a box. I mean, I couldn't be completely certain about that, but I thought I did. Even so, somehow it got onto the table, and I can't figure out how."

Jacob frowns, deep in thought. "Perhaps you put it there without remembering?"

I shake my head. "I don't see why I would. I went to bed last night, and it wasn't there. And when I woke this morning, it was."

He ponders this. "You don't sleepwalk, do you?"

I nod, sheepishly. "Well, yeah, I do have a habit of doing that but I don't know where I would have found that shirt, or why I would have put it on the table. It's not as if it was just lying around somewhere. I couldn't even tell you where it was, it's been packed away for so long."

He shrugs, and sips his coffee before answering. "I've read numerous times how people do the oddest things when sleepwalking, things that don't make any sense at all when they're awake. Perhaps you were just thinking of him, and your mind subconsciously led you to the shirt?"

That does make some sense, I guess.

But, it still doesn't feel quite right. I just can't shake the feeling that I'm missing something. Maybe I'm being paranoid and need to just let it go. Jacob is right—people do strange things when sleepwalking all the time. I've read about it before, too.

"You're probably right."

He steps forward, catching me around the waist and bringing me closer, grazing his lips over mine. "Try not to panic. I'm sure it's nothing at all. Don't get yourself flustered."

"Yeah, I know, but it just seems odd . . ."

"You're probably overreacting," he says carefully. "Honestly, it was likely something simple."

Am I overreacting? My brain twists even more. Maybe I am, it would make sense. I used to have strange dreams after Raymond died, and I'd find myself in odd places some mornings, like sleeping on the floor or sitting on the couch. It would make sense that I could do the same in this situation, too. After all, our anniversary was close, and I was thinking of him more than usual, especially considering I've kind of started dating again. Maybe that has stirred up a mix of feelings and brought it all to the surface.

"Yeah," I say softly. "No, you're right. I'm sure it's nothing. Thanks for bringing the coffee over. I really needed one."

"Oh I know," he chuckles. "I'm basically a mind reader."

I laugh and roll my eyes, nudging him with my shoulder. "What are your plans for today?"

He grins. "I'm taking you out for lunch, considering you told me you're working tonight, so go and get changed."

My heart warms a little. Getting out is just what I need to clear my head. "Sounds like a good plan. I won't be long."

I hurry off down the hall, and get changed for the day into some casual shorts and a light blue tee, then I pull my hair up into a ponytail after running a brush through it. I spray myself lightly with some body spray and then head back out. Jacob is sitting at my kitchen counter, studying his phone. He looks up when I come up, and his eyes lighten.

"You look nice."

I shift and flush. "Thanks. So, where are we going?"

He winks at me. "That's a surprise. Come on, let's get going or we'll be late."

Late.

Exciting.

I wonder where he's taking me.

SEVEN

I blink.

Then blink again, swallowing a few times before shaking my head to control my emotions.

What are the chances Jacob would bring me to the same place my husband not only asked me to marry him, but also the place where we actually held our wedding reception. I haven't been back here since he died. We used to come here often. It was *our* place, and I loved it. I haven't been able to come back. It was just too painful, and I honestly didn't think I'd be able to handle it without him.

"Is everything okay?" Jacob asks as I stare at the massive restaurant that overlooks thick woodland.

It's a gorgeous place.

And it serves some of the best food I've ever had.

I clear my throat, "Yes, of course. Sorry, it's just . . ."

I hesitate. Is it wrong to tell him that I used to come here with my husband? I don't want to make him uncomfortable, not in any way, but he does deserve to know the truth. I try not to talk a lot about Raymond on our dates, even though Jacob has asked a few times. I don't want to make it uncomfortable for him. Maybe I can suggest we can go somewhere else? That would make me feel a whole lot better. It's just not a place that I feel like I can share with someone else. It's just . . . it's Raymond's and my place.

It always will be.

Staring at the building, I can practically hear his happy laugh when I said yes after he got down on one knee. I can hear the slow drawl of his voice when he gave a toast at our reception, making everyone laugh and cry when he spoke about me. I can see the way his eyes held mine as we shared our first dance right there on the wooden deck that so many people are currently sitting on, enjoying their food.

Yes.

Our place. Our memories.

It's not Jacob's fault. He couldn't have had any idea what this place means to me, so in a soft voice I tell him, "It's just . . . I got married here."

Jacob is silent for a minute, and I look over at his face to see him studying the restaurant. Gosh, he probably feels so uncomfortable now. I know I would if I was in this situation. The poor guy probably feels terrible, but it isn't his fault.

"I didn't realize. I didn't know," he murmurs, looking down at me. "I'm so sorry, we can go somewhere else. But I do have a reservation and I've already paid for lunch . . ."

Dammit.

Dammit.

I know how hard it is to get a reservation here at Jade's Place, and their incredible prepaid three-course lunches are nonrefundable. It's why they're so popular, and they're one of few places that can get away with charging people ahead of time. I'd feel terrible if Jacob lost his money. It has been four years since I lost Ray, I have to face it eventually.

My heart clenches unhappily, but I force a smile.

"Of course, no,—of course we'll stay here," I say quickly, even though it just doesn't feel right.

Jacob smiles tentatively. "Are you sure?"

Seeing the hope on his face makes me feel more confident in my decision. "Absolutely." I'll just get through this the best I can.

He reaches for my hand and takes me inside the restaurant, speaking to a waitress about our table. I'm in somewhat of a daze as I glance around the beautiful restaurant. I've forgotten how incredible it is in here, how utterly breathtaking. Wooden booths, sleek floors, big glass windows that overlook acres of trees and mountains. The smell of food trails out, and my stomach grumbles.

"This way," the waitress says leading us to a table.

As we near, my heart clenches. *It can't be.* How is it possible that not only would Jacob bring me to this restaurant, but we would sit at the exact table Raymond proposed to me at? This is just too much. We stop and my knees tremble a little as Jacob pulls a chair out for me.

"Isn't the view spectacular? I requested this table specifically because they said it has the best view." I don't let on that I'm screaming inside. This isn't his fault. He's gone to such an effort for me, I need to stop being such a baby and suck it up.

So I sit down, even though everything inside of me is twisting in pain.

"What can I get you both to drink?" the waitress asks.

"Just a Coke for me, please," I say to her, my voice a little shakier than I'd like.

"Me too," Jacob says.

When she's gone, he looks over to me. "Are you okay? You've gone a little pale."

"Yeah, of course," I force out. "It's just been a long time since I've been here."

"I'm sorry," he says, eyes holding mine, and I can see genuine concern there. "If I had known, I wouldn't have brought you here. I've just heard such good things about it, I wanted to do something nice for you."

Dammit.

I'm sure this is awkward for him. There is no need for my mood to make it worse. My memories with Raymond will always be fond, but it doesn't mean I can't make some new ones. Being weird with Jacob isn't going to help. He's done a nice thing, I need to get over it. "It was a wonderful idea, thank you."

He smiles. "I hope you like seafood. I ordered the three-course seafood lunch."

I nod, my chest easing just a little. "Yes, I love it. It's my favorite."

He beams, again. "I'm a fan myself."

We talk casually for the next two hours while they bring out the three-course lunch: lobster tails, prawns, seafood chowder, and fresh bread rolls. It's amazing, and tastes as incredible as it always did. I stay a little uptight the entire time, but do my best to make the conversation flow. He's gone to so much effort. I can't deny that I breathe a little easier when we step outside of the restaurant to leave.

"You're really not happy, are you?" he says to me on the car ride home.

I've just shifted in the seat, trying to ease my discomfort. I ate far too much. I'm not entirely sure if that was because I was hungry, or if I was trying to hide from the awkward tension between Jacob and me, because my mood wasn't quite right.

"I'm okay, honestly."

He gives me a sideways look. "You were slightly off during lunch."

I swallow. "I did my best. I'm sorry if I upset you, I wasn't trying to."

"A little," he admits, shrugging. "I know it was your place with your husband, but I honestly didn't know that, and I went to a big effort to plan everything."

Great.

Now I look like an asshole, and worse, I feel like one too.

"Maybe you can come over for dinner tomorrow night," I suggest, hoping that'll make up for things. "I'll make you something. To make up for it?"

He looks to me, sighs, and then nods. "Okay."

Gosh. I hope I don't ruin this before it even has a chance to launch. I don't want it to go badly. I really like Jacob.

I exhale. I can do this.

I can.

Dammit.

I stare at the faucet in my bathroom that started

as a slow leak and is now proceeding to get bigger and bigger by the second. I've tried stopping it, tried tightening the tap, but nothing is working. I've left four messages with the landlord, and three with Jacob, but it would seem nobody is available to help me. The water is already leaking over the sink, and I'm going to end up with a huge bill if it keeps up, not to mention the noise is driving me crazy.

I'll never be able to sleep with that sound trickling into my room.

With an exhale, my eyes flick to the left. There is another man on this floor who could help me, but the idea of going and asking him makes me cringe. Still, he's the only option right now, unless I call a plumber, but that's going to cost me, considering it's after hours. I have a big test tomorrow, and it's already well past ten. I need to make sure I get some sleep.

So, with pursed lips, I trudge out of my apartment and hesitantly move down the hall, praying he's not asleep, partially hoping he's not home, but mostly just wondering if he'll even help me out. We don't exactly like each other a great deal. I reach his door, hesitate, then knock. A few moments pass and nothing happens, so with a muttered curse, I knock harder.

Put some force into it, Hart.

I hear the click of the lock, and the door swings open. Ace is standing in the doorway, wearing nothing but a pair of long pajama bottoms that sit low on his hips, showing off that amazing body. And oh, what an incredible body it is. I mentally growl at myself to keep my eyes on his, when all I want to do is let them dip lower, to take a good look at those unbelievable biceps, those hard pecs, and those washboard abs.

But I don't.

That would be rude.

"Can I help you?" he murmurs, scratching the scruff on his chin where the dark shadow of a few days' growth can be clearly seen.

It's most definitely ready for a shave, but it's also kind of hot. It only makes him look broodier.

"I'm sorry to bother you," I begin, and then roll my eyes at my own statement before continuing. "But, I, ah, need some help."

He stares at me.

I wait.

He looks up to the ceiling, then back to me. "You going to tell me what you need help with, or are you going to stand there and just stare at me?"

Right. Dammit.

"I was waiting for you to answer."

I cross my arms.

He crosses his.

Our eyes lock.

"Lady, I'm tired. I have a bed waitin' for me that I would much rather be in then standing here dealing with you. Now, I repeat, are you going to tell me what you need help with, or are you going to just stand there?"

That kind of hurts, and hits me right in the chest. I didn't want to bother him for this very reason. Embarrassment floods me, and then anger quickly takes its place.

"You know what?" I mutter. "I'll deal with it myself. Sorry to bother you."

I turn and rush off back down the hall, shutting

my apartment door. I make a frustrated sound in my throat, and then sigh and make my way back to the bathroom. I'll put a towel underneath the now heavily leaking tap, at least that might stop the noise enough for me to be able to get some sleep. I feel slightly stupid for reacting the way I just did, because it probably would have been easier if I had just come out and said it.

But Ace gets me hot under the collar. Dammit.

"Out of the way."

I flinch and squeal at the masculine voice behind me, and spin around to see Ace standing in my doorway, wearing a black shirt now, and looking more than a little pissed off. Obviously I didn't lock my door. Obviously he didn't take me storming off as a hint that I no longer want his help.

"It's uncouth to enter someone's house without knocking."

I just said "uncouth." Kill me now. I'm digging this hole deeper and deeper with every passing second.

"I knocked," he mutters, walking over, taking me by the shoulders and quite literally lifting me out of the way. I try to hide the flush in my cheeks as his big arms move me with little to no effort. "You were too busy muttering about me to hear."

Was I muttering about him?

Probably.

"Right," I murmur. "Sorry, about, ah, yelling at you."

My cheeks burn, but I did overreact . . . just a little.

He ignores me, fiddling with the tap, before leaning down and glancing under the sink and fumbling around there for a few minutes, too. Then he straightens, turns, and doesn't look at me as he says, "I'll be back in a few minutes with some things to fix this. Don't lock the door or I will kick it down."

I flip him off as he walks out of the bathroom.

"I saw that," he mutters, before disappearing down the hall.

Surely he didn't see that. I grin, and I'd nearly bet he's grinning too.

The second he's gone, I go into the bathroom and move any unmentionables out of the way, like the lacy panties hanging from the towel rack and the tampons on the sink. That is a little too much for the detective to see, I think.

He returns a few minutes later with a tool set and some clear plastic packet filled with tiny little black rubber things. I step out of his way, and watch as he places it all down and starts messing around with the tap. My eyes slide to his arms as he moves, watching those biceps flex. Oh boy. That's hot. It should be illegal for men to have arms like that.

Especially jerky men.

After about half an hour, he steps away from the sink, turns both taps on and off, and then glances at me in the mirror. I'm still standing by the door, and when our eyes meet, I feel it right down to my toes. God, he's intense. Far too intense for my liking. Okay, that's a little bit of a lie. Maybe if he were nicer, I wouldn't be so taken aback by his intensity. I might even like it.

"It's fixed," he says, still staring at me. "Anything else you need while I'm here?"

"No, thank you."

His jaw tics a little, maybe out of surprise that I didn't throw some sarcastic comment his way. "If that starts leaking again, let me know."

He turns around, picking up his things and striding right past me and into the hall. I turn, rolling my eyes, and follow him out. He places his tools down onto my kitchen counter, and washes his hands in my sink.

Sure, make yourself right at home. I wonder if I should offer him a drink? I mean, he did fix my sink, and I'm always telling him he has no manners. Besides, he'd never say yes. The man can't stand me.

"Do you want a drink, or, ah, something?"

That sounded convincing.

His eyes flick to me, and he wipes his hands dry on his pants. "Coffee would be good."

Dammit.

He accepted.

Now what do I do?

My heart races for a minute, and I just stare at him. He stares right back. Right. Coffee. Simple enough. I shake myself from my stupor and head towards the counter, avoiding his eyes as I turn the coffee maker on. I grab one cup, because there is no way I'm drinking coffee before bed, and start preparing it for him.

"Doesn't coffee keep you awake?" I ask, looking over my shoulder at him.

He's on the other side of the counter now, leaning a hip against it.

"I work most of the night, so no."

Right, he's a detective. I can only imagine how much time he spends poring over cases, trying to figure things out. It would be a job where you couldn't turn your mind off all that easily. The things he would see in his line of work would keep most people awake for the rest of their lives, I imagine.

"Understandable," I murmur. "Anything interesting you're working on right now?"

"I'm working on a few homicide cases."

I blink and turn, while the coffee brews. "You are?"

He nods.

Wow. That's impressive, and kind of cool.

"Did you hear about the recent killing? That killer?"

He nods. "Yeah, it isn't my case so I haven't looked much into it, but I have seen a few like that pass through over the years."

"Are they any closer to finding the person responsible?"

I'm so curious, even though he probably can't answer me.

He shakes his head. "Serial killers are always tricky, a lot of the time we just don't get them. They're usually calculated and smart as hell, so we basically have to wait for them to screw up and if they don't, then we're left in a difficult position. They're not reckless like most killers, they're smarter than most of the human population, which makes it tricky."

I shiver. "That's a scary thought . . . you know . . . that you're waiting on someone to screw up just to catch them."

I finish up his coffee and slide it to him, "Cream in the fridge, sugar in the pantry."

I take a seat at the counter and watch him move around, taking the coffee and helping himself to my fridge. He mixes three spoons of sugar into the cup, and nothing else. Black and sweet. Interesting. When he takes a seat again, he tells me, "Serial killers tend to be extremely clever, and they do a lot of research before targeting anyone. It's why they're so hard to catch. I've only ever heard of a few that aren't up there with the rest—most of them are near-genius level."

"Hmmmm," I ponder thoughtfully. "Yeah, I can see what you're saying. I've seen all those serial killer movies."

He looks to the ceiling. I am starting to notice he seems to do that a lot when he's frustrated. How my comment frustrates him, however, I don't know. "The movies are fiction . . ."

I snort. "I'm fully aware of that, but they do hold some truth."

Don't they?

His eyes swing to me and I swear—I swear—he rolls them a little.

"You're not a very easy person to communicate with, are you, Detective?"

He studies me. "I could say the same about you, Hartley."

I blink. "How do you know my name?"

He keeps staring at me. "I know all I need to know about you. I did a background check when you moved in."

My mouth drops open. "That's an invasion of privacy!"

He shrugs. "I didn't want to be living next door to someone who's a criminal."

I'm shaking my head, even as the words keep pouring out of my mouth. "You, buddy, need to learn some serious people skills. It is not okay to do background checks on people. That's my business."

He gives me a look that says *I beg to differ*. "I'm a cop. It's mine, too."

God.

I want to punch him right between the eyes.

I don't know why he frustrates me so much, but gosh, he does. He really really does.

"It's not normal for neighbors to check on other neighbor's private business," I point out. "Not that you seem to be overly concerned about being neighborly."

He snorts, taking a big gulp of coffee. "I don't do neighborly things."

"You fixed my tap," I add with a smile. "That's neighborly."

He gives me a look that tells me he really had no choice in the matter. "Because you came to my house, threw a tantrum, and I had no choice."

My mouth drops open. "I did *not* throw a tantrum."

His brows go up, as if to say *Oh really*?

I grind my teeth. "Well, considering you've stalked me, I figure it's only fair that I'm allowed one act of kindness from you."

"I didn't stalk you," he says, standing and putting his cup in the sink. "I did a background check."

So he knows about Raymond?

He probably knows everything about me.

Not weird at all.

"Same difference," I mumble, walking to the door and holding it open for him. "I have to get some sleep, I have a test tomorrow. Thanks for doing your yearly neighborly duties and helping me."

Unfazed by my little jab, he leans down, picks up his tools, walks to the door and steps out into the hall. "Keep an eye on that tap."

With that, he strolls off back to his apartment.

I can't help but give a little smile.

EIGHT

I blink, once, twice, and then sit up in bed. A sound can be heard faintly traveling through my apartment. I rub my eyes and listen. It sounds like a video is playing somewhere, maybe a television, or the radio. If I listen hard enough, it almost sounds like people talking, but it seems too close for me to be able to hear it that clearly.

In all the time I've lived here, I've never heard any noise from outside my own apartment. These apartments are soundproof, or maybe it's just that my neighbors are quiet. Either way, it's always quiet. It almost sounds like it's inside the apartment.

I glance at the clock. It's seven a.m.

I studied all day yesterday, and well into the night, not slipping into bed until midnight. Jacob brought me lunch during the day, keeping me entertained for a little while, but eventually I had to get back to it. I was exhausted when I fell asleep, I don't even think I got up to use the toilet. I rub my eyes again and climb out of bed in search of the sound that woke me.

I move into the hall and towards the living room. With every step I take, the sound gets louder and louder, until I'm standing in my living room, staring at my television, my body stiff and my heart racing. This must be a dream. It has to be. I know, I just know, that what is playing on the television right now was packed away a long time ago. I know because I cried so many tears as I watched it one final time, then wrapped it and sealed the box. I remember it like it was yesterday, the way my heart felt like it was being torn from my chest as I said good bye to my husband for a final time.

"I, Hartley James, take you Raymond Watson to be my husband."

My voice trails out from the speakers on the TV and I can't drag my eyes from the screen, from Raymond's smiling face, from the tears in my eyes. This has to be some sort of joke. It has to be. There is no other way my wedding video would be playing. I didn't put it in there. I didn't. I would know if I did. There is no way I'd put myself through the pain of watching this again. Dragging my eyes from the TV, I rush down the hall to the spare room.

The box the video was in, has been opened, but sealed back shut. Did I do that? I try to think back and recall if I have opened these boxes recently, but I can't seem to remember doing that.

Something isn't right.

In a panic, I turn the video off and rush back out and dial Taylor right away, trying to calm my racing heart. I'm either losing my mind, or something is very wrong. How and why would my wedding video be playing? Is this some sort of joke? Some sort of trick? I'm sure I didn't sleepwalk last night. I was so tired and nothing else in my apartment is messed up or different. No. Something is off. I know it. I can feel it. My palms start sweating as I say over and over, "Come on. Answer."

"Hey, babes," she answers on the fifth ring.

"Taylor," I croak. "Something is wrong."

Her happy tone instantly turns worried. "Shit, Hart, are you okay? What's happened?"

I stammer over quickly what has happened, how I found Raymond's shirt, and now our wedding video is playing. It's all too much for me, and I'm freaking out. I can't control it. I'm trying but I can't. I close my eyes and take a staggering breath when I'm done, waiting for her to respond. Praying she will have some valid explanation that makes it all better.

"Honey, calm down. I know it seems weird, but is it possible that you may have actually been sleepwalking both of those times?"

I take a deep breath.

Calm.

Be calm.

"I'd know if I was sleepwalking," I say, my voice still thick and full of emotion.

"People don't," she says, her voice so calming, so steady. "Some have left their houses and not known it. Hell, there are those people that even eat full meals in their sleep. It is highly possible you're subconsciously doing these things. Have you been thinking about Raymond more than usual lately?

Possibly you dating Jacob has stirred up some old feelings, maybe even some guilty ones, and it has brought it all to the surface?"

I close my eyes, and think about her question. I mean, sure I've been thinking about him more often lately, but I've also been really enjoying myself with Jacob, and I thought I had the guilt under control. I feel okay about moving on. I really do. So why would it be affecting me so much?

"Sure," I admit. "I mean, I guess Ray has been on my mind more than normal, but I have felt mostly okay with it."

"Still, it is a big step," she says, calmly. "It's possible that this is a reaction to you finally moving on. It's probably normal—remember in college you did it a few times when we were sharing a room."

"I'm sure you're right. I remember that night when I sleepwalked out into the hall and someone was trying to talk to me." I take another breath. "So, you're probably right, I have done strange things in my sleep before. It just freaks me out and I can't really figure out why. The logical explanation says that you're right and I'm overreacting, that makes the most sense, but for some reason, I just can't shake the worry."

"It would freak anyone out. Maybe go and see the therapist you saw after Raymond died, if you're concerned. She might be able to help you make more sense of it, but from an outsider's point of view, it kind of seems normal. You're closing that chapter of your life, and inside you're probably feeling that a little."

"Yeah," I say distractedly. "Yeah, no, you're right."

"Try not to stress, hon. The more you stress, the harder it'll get for you."

"Thanks, Tay. I don't know what I'd do without you."

"Well, you probably wouldn't sleepwalk, for a start . . ."

I laugh softly. She always knows how to make me feel better. Even during the most difficult times, she knows what to say.

"I'll call you later. I have a big day ahead, I just needed someone to calm me down. Thank you."

"I'm always here, you know that," she says, her voice soft. "Later, honey."

"Laters."

I hang up the phone and walk back into the living room, staring at the television screen. My eyes burn as I watch Raymond and me on the screen, so happy, so in love. He was the best man I've ever known, and I know I'll miss him until the day I die. That doesn't mean one day I won't love again—I'm sure I will—but Raymond certainly set the bar high. He was incredible. With trembling hands, I walk over and pull the video out, taking it back to the box and sealing it once again.

Sleepwalking.

Could that really be what's happening?

Why does my gut tell me there's more to it?

NINE

"So it happened again?" Jacob asks, sipping his coffee as we sit across from each other at breakfast the morning after my big test.

"Yeah," I shrug. "I don't honestly remember anything, I just know that the video was playing when I woke up."

He purses his lips, deep in thought. "And you're concerned about it?"

I purse my lips, too, and then nod. "I'm a little worrie—I mean, what if it isn't me doing it . . ."

His brows knit together. "You think someone is doing it on purpose?"

"That sounds stupid when you say it out loud," I mumble, staring down at my plate of untouched scrambled eggs.

"Can I get you another coffee?" the waitress asks as she passes.

Both of us decline, and she continues on her way without another word. She's been too busy smiling and flirting with the group of men sitting at the next table to pay too much attention to us.

"It's not stupid," Jacob assures me, reaching over and patting my hand. "How is your security in that place?"

I give him a sheepish look. "It's not that great, I'll admit. I could probably break into my front door without a lot of effort, but I figure it's safe enough because it's in a good area, you know. And Ace lives right next door."

"Ace?" Jacob questions.

Right, I forgot I never told Jacob that I live next door to a detective, and one who can, more often than not, be a dick.

"Yeah, he's a detective. I don't have a great deal to do with him, though."

He nods, glancing down at his breakfast. He doesn't say anything for a moment, then he looks back up at me. "Well, if you don't mind, I'd like to change your locks for you. It'll make both you and me feel safer. Is that okay?"

My heart flutters. That's sweet. He cares enough to make sure that I not only *feel* safer, but *am* safer. "That's kind, thank you."

He smiles, and continues with his breakfast. When we're done, we go down to the local hardware shop and get some new locks and keys, and then we head back to my apartment. We're just through the front doors when I see Ace coming out of the elevator and making his way towards us. He stops when he notices us. He's fully dressed for work, but I would have thought he went to work earlier. Maybe he came home for something.

He must have needed to come home for something.

His eyes scan over Jacob, and I could swear his lip curls a little. God. He is such a dick when he wants to be. He doesn't even know the man and he's giving him a look like he wants to flick him away like some sort of annoying bug. I exhale and walk towards him, stopping in front of him and tipping my head back just slightly to look up at him. "Ace, it's nice to see you again. This is my friend, Jacob."

Ace studies me, eyes dropping to my lips, and then flicking over to Jacob. "What are the locks for?"

I cringe.

No *Hello*.

No *Pleased to meet you*.

Just demands. Always with the demands.

"I wanted to change Hart's locks," Jacob says, his voice gruff, too. "Her old ones aren't very good."

Ace keeps staring at him, narrowing his eyes. "Yes, I'm aware."

Sheesh.

This man really has no tact, at all.

"So I'm changing them," Jacob retorts. "She doesn't feel safe."

Ace looks back to me. "You never told me you weren't feeling safe."

He's acting like we're friends, and I should have told him this information.

This man confuses the hell out of me.

"No offense," I say, my voice a little snippy. "But

I think I've had one decent conversation with you. I don't know why you think I'd tell you that."

He scowls at me.

I scowl right back.

Then he nods, and starts walking. Like we didn't just have that conversation. He just dismisses Jacob and me, without even a good bye. Gosh. The insults I want to hurl at him right now are bubbling in my chest, just waiting to explode out, but I keep them in.

"God, he's a dick," I mutter, turning to Jacob. "Sorry about that."

Jacob is watching him go, and only when Ace is out the front doors, does he turn to me. "That jerk is your neighbor?"

"Sadly, yes."

He exhales. "I feel sorry for you. He's an ass. Come on, let's get these locks changed up for you. I'm starting to see it'll make *me* feel better, too."

I nod and follow him to my apartment, unlocking the front door. Jacob gets to work pulling the old locks off, and replacing them with the new ones. When he's done, he hands me a set of keys. "New keys. If you have any problems with them, give me a call. Hopefully you'll feel safer now."

I smile at him. "Thank you, I really appreciate it."

He winks, and then extends a hand and takes mine, pulling me closer. I let him bring me in for a hug, and he leans down, sweeping his lips across mine.

"I have to get back to work," he murmurs. "I really don't want to, but I have to. I'll call you later."

"Okay," I say softly, staring up at him through my lashes.

"Bye, Hartley."
"Later, Jacob."
I watch him go, smiling.
Yeah, he's a good one.

TEN

"That douche your boyfriend?"

I turn at the sound of a voice coming from behind me just as I'm opening my apartment door after doing a shift at the hospital for my training. I haven't seen Ace in the few days since Jacob and I ran into him. I didn't even see him there, honestly, I wasn't paying any attention at all. I usually hear him, but I've been off in my own little world the last few days. I can't really explain why, but my mind is just so distracted.

"Jacob?"

He shrugs. "Yeah. Is he your boyfriend or not?"

"Why?"

He looks to the ceiling.

Impatient, isn't he?

"Can you just answer a question without being sarcastic?"

Oh. Snappy.

"Not that it's any of your business, but I am dating him, yes."

Ace snorts.

"What's the damned problem?" I snap at him, putting my hands on my hips.

He curls his lip. Obviously, he doesn't like Jacob. "He's a weasel."

God.

"And you say that after only meeting him once? Where you didn't even acknowledge his presence?"

Ace just stares at me, unapologetically.

"He's a nice man," I go on. "Unlike you."

He keeps staring.

"He does things for me . . . like fixes my locks . . . and takes me out . . ."

Now I sound pathetic.

"Who are you trying to convince? Me or yourself?"

Grrrr.

"I swear, Ace, I'm seriously considering coming over there and fly kicking you in the damned face."

He crosses his arms. "I'd like to see that."

"What is your problem?" I cry, throwing my hands up. "Seriously, can't you just be nice?"

"I am being nice."

"Oh my god!" I say, my eyes rolling to the ceiling. "Screw it."

I shove my door open and step inside, slamming it with all my might. It doesn't make me feel any better, not really, but I'm still satisfied that he would have heard the booming and felt it right to his bones, the jackass. Exhaling, I lock the door and walk into the kitchen, dumping my stuff down. I need wine. Stat. I need something to help me unwind, because honestly, I feel so uptight right now. I need to relax.

I pour a glass for myself, topping it up after every few sips. I kick off my shoes, change into something comfortable—small cotton shorts and a tank—and then I kick back on the sofa and continue drinking the wine. It goes down way too well, and before I know it, I've polished off half the bottle. My body is relaxed and I sink back into the chair, exhaling.

The power goes out.

I swear, one minute everything is bright and the next I'm thrust into pitch-black. For a moment, I just sit there, then I burst into hysterical laughter. As if everything that's happened in the last few days hasn't been enough, now this on my one night where I can enjoy myself, and sleep in tomorrow. Of course this would happen.

There's a pounding at my door, and my head whips over in its general direction. I'm still laughing hysterically, far beyond tipsy, as I stumble towards the small strip of light coming from beneath the gap in the door. I reach it—slam into it, actually—face squashing against the wood. It stops my laughter for a brief second as an uncomfortable pain shoots up my nose, and then I go right back to giggling again. Finally I unlock the door and fling it open.

Ace is standing there, flashlight pointed to the ground. I can just see his face in the light bouncing off the floor. He looks . . . well . . . like he always looks. Moody.

"I'm still alive, if that's what you're here checking," I giggle.

One brow cocks. "Are you drunk?"

"Tipsy."

"Same difference."

"Actually," I smirk, "there is a difference."

He grunts. "I was checking if you'd lost power, too. I guess we're all out."

I giggle. "You were checking if I was still alive, admit it. You want to be my friend."

"Jesus," he mumbles under his breath. "Have you got a flashlight in there? I'm not going to ask if you've got candles because I'd prefer not to die tonight when you burn the entire apartment complex down because you're drunk."

"Are you always this dramatic or am I the only lucky one that gets to experience it?"

I'm sure if I could see, he'd be rolling his eyes. I smile. "Where are your flashlights?"

I shrug, though I'm not sure he can see it. "I'm not really sure, it's been a long time since we've had a power outage."

"Okay, go and sit on the sofa, I'll find you one."

"No. I'll help you look."

A deep sound graces that throat, and then he sighs. "Okay, where would you normally keep them?"

I try to think of where I'd most likely put my flashlights, but I haven't really needed them. So I guess I'd store them somewhere out of the way. I'm guessing the spare room.

"Probably in the spare room. We can start there."

Ace locks my door, and then we move down the hall and I shove open the spare room door. I reach for the light, only to realize it isn't going to work. Well, I guess we're sharing a flashlight, then. I reach over for the one Ace is holding, but he jerks his hand back. "No. I'll hold it."

Bossy.

"Well, shine it around then, we're not going to see anything if you keep it pointed at the floor."

He shines the flashlight around the room, and we move to the cabinet I have in the corner. It has heaps of pens, stationery, paper, things like that in it. There might be a flashlight stashed in there somewhere. I open drawers and start rifling through it while Ace holds the light over everything, so I can see. We come up empty, so I move to Raymond's old desk, which is in the corner and piled up with crap.

I could never bring myself to sell it, but I couldn't bring myself to use it, either. So it just sits there, collecting dust.

I start shoving things aside when my hand freezes, extended in front of me, like I'm reaching for something.

I blink. Then I blink again. No. It can't be. I shake my head, wondering if I'm just imagining things, if the alcohol is making me see things that aren't there, but I know I'm not. I'd know that laptop anywhere. Raymond used to take it everywhere with him. I haven't been able to find it—I know because I went searching through the boxes only a few months ago, looking.

I couldn't remember where I put it.

I know for a fact it was not sitting on the desk . . . open.

My heart lodges into my throat. Maybe I could believe it was sleepwalking when it was just a few small things, but this . . . not even someone sleepwalking could have found this easily. No way in the world. Something is wrong. Something is definitely wrong. I tremble, my hand is still extended out in front of me, and for a second I have forgotten Ace is standing right next to me.

"Hartley?"

His voice is probably the kindest I've ever heard it, but even then it still holds a sharp edge.

I can't move.

I honestly can't move.

What is happening right now?

"Hartley?"

Ace again.

My hand falls, dropping to my side, and I whisper, "Ace, something is wrong."

It's not much of an explanation, and honestly, I don't know why I'm even telling him, because he's been nothing but a dick to me, but he is a cop, and whatever is happening right now, it isn't right. One thing, I can overlook; two, I can brush off; but this . . . no. No. Something is very, very wrong.

"You're not making any sense. Hey, look at me."

I look over to him, and my eyes meet his.

"I think someone has been in my house."

I stare at the floor, suddenly starkly sober, trying to get my mind in order, trying to figure out why someone would be trying to mess with me, and who that might be. Because that's what they're doing, right? They're messing with me. Why else would someone place things from my husband all around my house? There is no valid explanation. None whatsoever. Except that someone is doing it on purpose. But who? Why?

Raymond couldn't have done this, could he? I mean, is this some sort of *P.S. I Love You* reenactment? No. If it was Raymond, it would have happened earlier. This is just too off for it to be some old supernatural romantic gesture coming to the surface.

"Tell me what's been happening," Ace says, sitting on the sofa across from me.

The power came back on a couple of minutes ago, and we came out here. I open my mouth, and I know he's not going to leave now until I tell him what I know. Will he think I'm crazy? Am I going crazy? I don't know if I'm overreacting, or if this is a real thing. I don't know what to think, to be completely honest. It's all just too . . . strange.

"Well, I first noticed something off when I found a shirt of Raymond's, my deceased husband, on the kitchen table one morning. I was sure I'd packed the shirt away, but I have a history of sleepwalking, so I figured maybe I'd come across it and placed it there without knowing. Then I woke up one morning, and my wedding video was playing right there on my television. Again, I wondered if I had somehow put it on myself . . ."

"Do you often do things when sleepwalking?" Ace asks, cutting me off.

I give him a look, but his face is serious and I realize he's not being rude, so I answer him honestly. "Well, Taylor, my best friend, told me I did it a few times in college. Raymond never mentioned it. I have been known to get out of bed, and I've sometimes found myself sleeping in odd places, but I've never actually moved things, as far as I know. But I have been thinking of Raymond more of late, and I wondered if maybe he was playing on my mind and that would explain why I was gravitating towards his things."

He seems skeptical, and that only makes my heart clench more. "But you saw something in that office tonight that made you second guess."

I meet Ace's eyes. "His laptop. I haven't been able to find it anywhere, I went through all my boxes, all my things, and couldn't find it. That's not to say it wasn't here—it could have been stored somewhere I didn't look—but the thing is, if I couldn't find it awake, what are the chances of me finding it sleepwalking?"

Ace is deep in thought as he stares at me, then he murmurs, "Anything else been happening? Strange phone calls? Anyone talking to you on the street? Anything out of the ordinary at all?"

I think about that for a minute, but no, I can't think of anything else that might count as strange.

"I went on a few dates recently, but honestly, I feel like they were normal enough to not do something like this."

Ace nods, studying me. "I'd like their names, just to be safe."

I nod back, frowning.

"Is it possible you've sleepwalked and actually done all of this? Really ask yourself, is that something you believe to be possible, at all?"

I do as he asks, I really think about it, I dig deep into the depths of my soul. And the answer is the same. I don't honestly believe it's all sleepwalking. I haven't truly believed that from the start. I know something isn't right, I can feel it right in the pit of my belly. I just wanted to put it down to something simple because I felt like that would make more sense, but the fact of the matter is, I just know it isn't simple.

Something is off, I just don't know what it is.

I meet and hold his eyes. "No. For the first few things, I could brush it off, but—this is going to sound stupid—my gut just felt . . . I don't know how to explain it, but something just didn't feel right."

Ace nods, and then pulls out his phone, typing something in. "I'm going to make some calls in the morning, see if I can find anything out. I'll talk to security in this place, see if they've picked up anything. Is there anyone else you can think of, anyone at all, who might be doing this? No friends thinking it would be funny to play a joke on you?"

I shake my head right away. "I don't know anyone that would be that cruel, and that's the honest truth. I haven't met anyone new outside of those few dates I mentioned."

"And you're sure they didn't feel off to you?"

I purse my lips. "They were a little weird, but not in a stalker, come-into-your-house kind of way. One was a little obsessed with younger women, and did message me on social media apologizing for being shallow, but I don't feel he was a bad man, you know?"

Ace nods again, and tucks his phone away. "I'd still like all their details. Do you feel safe sleeping here tonight?"

I hadn't thought of that, but the second he asks the question, my chest tightens. I'm not sure I do feel safe sleeping here, thinking that someone might have been in my house, or worse, someone is trying to torment me in some way. I mean, if there is someone behind this, then they've been in my house . . . while I was in it. That thought does not make me feel good inside, at all.

"Not really."

"You got anyone you can call?"

I could call Taylor, though she's probably working, considering she's a nurse and works strange hours. That leaves Jacob. Is it too soon to call him? Would that seem weird to ask for his help? I don't know. We're casually dating, and I really like him, but the passion is hardly exploding out of the room. I'm certainly not ready to go "there" with him yet—would he think that if I asked him to come and stay over?

Ace must sense my hesitation, because he stands, crossing his arms and then uncrossing them. "I'll be back in ten."

I blink up at him. "I beg your pardon?"

"I'll. Be. Back. In. Ten."

"Why?" I whisper-hiss.

"To sleep on your damned couch until the morning, when I can sort out your security properly and figure out what's going on."

I gape at him. "No. No way."

Those eyes roll to the ceiling again. "Woman, you're testing all my patience. I'm a cop. This is what we do. If anyone can keep you safe for one night, it's me."

I give him a skeptical look. "You could be anyone . . . how do I know you're really a cop?"

He gives me a truly scathing look. "I'll bring my badge over, if you insist."

"Just because you're a cop, doesn't mean you're

not . . . I don't know . . . some kind of killer, or rap-
ist, or—"

"Fuck. Me."

I blink again. "Seriously, does it have to be you?"

He exhales, clearly trying to gather some patience.
"Do you want someone here, or not? I'm happy to
leave you and your sassy mouth here on your own,
if that makes you feel better."

Dammit, it doesn't.

It really doesn't.

I sigh. "Fine, but I'm locking my bedroom door."

He stares at me, then shakes his head and walks
out of my house muttering.

Great. Just great.

ELEVEN

I toss and turn in my bed—left to right, right to left, onto my stomach, onto my back—finally I sigh and sit up.

I can't sleep, there is just no way it's coming to me tonight. Not when I know Ace is out there sleeping on my couch. How is anyone supposed to concentrate with that kind of distraction? I pull my phone from the bedside table and glance down at the time. It's just past three. I shoot a quick text to Taylor, knowing she's at work.

H: You awake?

A minute later, a response comes through.

T: Yep. On a break. You're a creeper texting me just as I sat down. Why are you awake so early?
H: Don't freak out . . .

T: Oh my god. I'm freaking out! What! What is
　it! Speak!
H: Ace is on my couch.

A minute ticks by. Then another.

Then my phone rings. I answer it with a soft laugh, not because I'm actually feeling good, but because only Taylor would ring that quickly given such news.

"Tell me right now why he's on your couch?" she demands. "I swear I've only got a few minutes so you better speak fast, woman!"

"He's here because some more weird things have been happening. I found Raymond's laptop tonight, and I know for a fact it was not where I found it— someone put it there. In fact, I don't remember the last time I saw it. So, I didn't really want to be left alone, and there weren't many people we could call, so . . . he stayed."

"Oh, honey, that's awful. Are you okay?"

"Yeah, kind of. I feel a little better knowing Ace is here."

"So he's on your couch . . ."

"Yes." I laugh. "On my couch."

"I didn't think you even liked him that much."

I snort. "We didn't really see eye to eye, but he's a cop and he knows what he's doing, you know? It seemed like the logical thing to do."

"Right, logical."

I roll my eyes, even though she can't see it. "Be quiet. I feel safer, at least."

She makes a concerned sound. "So you don't think you were sleepwalking then?"

I exhale slowly. "I'm starting to think maybe I wasn't. It doesn't make a lot of sense. I mean, the shirt maybe, but the rest of it . . ."

Taylor makes another noise in her throat. "It does seem odd, doesn't it? I just don't understand why anyone would do something like that. I mean, they obviously have to have known you were married, and that you lost your husband, so why would they do that?"

I wonder that myself. "That's what I'm trying to figure out. To think someone is doing it on purpose makes absolutely no sense and it just keeps leading me back to the fact that maybe I am sleepwalking . . ."

"Possibly, but, I don't know . . . it still doesn't seem to be adding up, does it?"

I exhale and sigh. "No."

"Anyway, honey, I'd love to talk more but I really do need to get back to work. I'll pop around tomorrow, after I've had a sleep, and see how you're doing, okay?"

"Okay, love you."

"Love you too."

I hang up the phone and climb out of bed. I tiptoe down the hall and into the kitchen, needing some water and trying not to make any noise. I glance over at the sofa, where Ace is sleeping so quietly you wouldn't even know he was there if his big body wasn't practically hanging off the sides. Poor guy. That can't be comfortable. I should probably be nicer to him.

He didn't have to stay, after all.

I study him while he's asleep, and notice he's not wearing that signature scowl. I wonder what happened to make him so broody? Is it just that he's got such a demanding job and it tires him out, or is it something else? I let my eyes roam over the edges of his perfectly masculine face. He's an exceptionally good-looking man, I can't deny that. He's the kind of man who sparks a fire in your soul.

He's the kind of man who, if you were dating, you'd always want to be with, just so you could feel what he makes you feel. He'd have passion raging in your body. It's written all over him. Raymond wasn't like that, and come to think of it, neither is Jacob. They're the good-looking, sweet, charming kind. Ace, he's the dangerous kind, the fierce protector, the man of very few words.

What would it be like to be loved by someone like him? I've never really thought about dating a man like him. I guess I never really knew many of them. I will admit it does spark my curiosity.

"Are you goin' to stare at me all night?"

I squeal and jump backwards at the gruff voice that sounds out of nowhere. What the hell? How did he know I was standing there looking at him? His eyes were closed. He barely moved. I blink a few times, and then say in a weak tone, "I wasn't staring!"

Even I don't believe it.

He probably thinks I really am crazy. Dammit.

"I can feel you," he grumbles, opening those eyes and looking directly at me. "You always stare at people when they sleep?"

I cross my arms, trying to pull out some sass, even though my heart is thudding against my rib cage. I can't really explain this one away, because, well, I was being a weirdo just standing there and staring at the poor guy. "I was just admiring the fact that you're so peaceful and kind-looking when you're sleeping. Probably something to do with the fact that you're not speaking."

He grunts, pushing up.

The blanket falls off, revealing that sculpted, perfectly toned body. My mouth goes dry and I try very very hard to avert my eyes. I mean, I've seen it before but it still renders me speechless. He has an incredible body—it's tight, and well formed, and smooth as hell. He has tattoos down both his arms, one running over his shoulder and his chest. I don't study them too closely, but they look like they might be some sort of skull design, with flames mixed in.

I swallow and turn quickly when he cocks an eyebrow at me.

I warm myself up a glass of milk and get the hell out of there before he sees the flush creeping up my cheeks.

"Seriously?" Jacob says, taking a seat at my kitchen counter. "Why didn't you call me?"

I give him a weak smile, shifting from foot to foot as I try to give him a valid explanation as to why I didn't call him, without offending him. "Well, to be honest, we're only new to this, ah, dating thing, and I didn't really think that would be okay at this point."

He stares at me, looking slightly offended. His eyes scan over my face for a moment, before he shrugs it off and says, "I guess I understand, but you can call me if you're in trouble. Please don't feel like you have to hesitate."

Right. Of course. Jacob is a nice guy, he probably wouldn't have even thought twice if I called him asking for help. Still, Ace is a cop and it makes more sense that he was here, just in case something else happened. At least, that explanation makes me feel better for not calling Jacob, because truthfully, I just really didn't want to, and I'm not entirely sure why that is.

"Yes, thank you. Next time, I promise to call you."

He winks at me, seemingly having let it go. "So what is the cop going to do?"

I shrug. "He said he would give me a call later. He's going to change the locks again, check the security on the building, just little things like that."

Jacob's face scrunches. "What's wrong with the locks I put on?"

Oh dear. I didn't think he might be offended by that.

"He just said he was going to put in bigger ones, maybe an extra latch. It's not that your locks aren't sufficient . . ."

Jacob narrows his eyes. "Are you sure he's not making this situation out to be worse than it is?"

I shake my head in confusion. "How do you mean?"

"Well, it is highly possible that you did sleepwalk. I know the laptop is a little above and beyond, but I don't want people putting ideas into your head, or making you think something that might not be right. Scaring you excessively might not be helping matters."

He's right, to a point. I've thought over and over how it just doesn't make sense that someone would do this, but I also don't understand how I could do all those things sleepwalking. I'm at war with myself, wondering if I'm making a big deal out of nothing, or if I'm not making a big enough deal about something serious. I honestly don't know.

"Have you considered at least going to see a therapist?"

A therapist.

I did consider it, but what can they do for sleepwalking? Give me drugs to knock me out so heavily I can't do it? No, that wouldn't make me feel good. I don't think that's going to solve anything.

"I have considered that."

His eyes scan my face. "I want you to do whatever makes you feel safe, Hart. If you feel like having the cop checking it all out does that, then I'm fine with it. I just don't want anyone to make a mountain out of a molehill . . . you have enough going on in your life."

That's sweet. But, now I'm questioning myself. He has a point. Am I scaring myself for nothing?

Am I making too big a deal out of this?

Dammit. My head hurts.

"I mean"—Jacob laughs lightly,—"you can be a little clumsy. You did leave your keys in your car last week, and you have a habit of forgetting things."

He's right.

I do.

I feel uneasy now. Wondering if I am taking this too far.

"You're right. It's just right now, I feel uneasy . . ."

He smiles and raises a hand in a casual gesture.

"Of course. You do whatever feels safe. I don't like the idea that someone might have been in your apartment either, so I'm glad you're being cautious."

I shudder. "I'm also trying to figure out why anyone would even want to get into my apartment. It makes no sense to me."

He shakes his head. "No, it certainly doesn't. Not at all. What time is he changing the locks?"

"He said he is working long hours today, but will come and do it in the next few days. He's waiting for the locks to arrive. I'm okay with that. I'll double-check all the locks when I go to sleep each night until then."

Not that that makes me feel any better, because if someone has been getting in, they have been doing it regardless of the locks. I think maybe I should check the windows, too. Ace mentioned putting locks on them. We're not on ground level, but I don't think it would be hard for someone to climb up the fire escape and pry one of them open. But to do that without making any noise? I doubt it. I make a mental note to have a look when Jacob leaves, just to be sure.

"Do you need me to stay with you for a few days?"

My instinct is that I don't want him to stay, which I'm not sure is the right answer. I really like Jacob, I truly do, but we're only casually seeing each other right now. I'm not even sure you could classify us as being anything but friends who are seeing where it goes. We're not in a relationship, and I'm not ready to be, not at this stage at least. I don't want to offend him, I care about him a lot, but sleeping over seems like it'll be putting too much pressure where it doesn't need to be. Sometimes I feel like I'm not giving as much as he is. Maybe I need to put more effort in. Try harder. Can I truly say I'm not ready, when I'm not truly putting my best foot forward?

So I give him my best, casual smile and say, "Thanks, but Taylor is going to come and stay."

That's a valid enough explanation.

He nods, giving me a smile, seemingly unfazed. "Well, please call if you need anything. Honestly, I'm worried about you."

He's a good man. I walk over, reach out, and squeeze his arm. "Thank you, but I'll be fine."

He sighs and looks at his watch. "Okay then. I'd love to stay, but I have to get going. You'd never believe I designed a whole package for a client, only for her to change her mind on the colors at the last minute."

"Oh, that's awful! You'll have to show me some of your work sometime. I'd love to see it."

In fact, I don't even know where he lives.

Probably a good thing at this stage.

He nods, flashing me a grin. "Absolutely. I've got to run. Stay safe, lock that door, and just be careful of that cop. He makes me uneasy."

I blink.

Ace makes him uneasy? That's strange.

Ace is a lot of things, but he doesn't seem like a bad person.

It's interesting he gives Jacob a bad vibe. I make note of that, too.

"I will. Thank you, Jacob."

He stands and walks over, brushing his lips across my temple. "I'll call you later."

He leaves my apartment and I lock the door behind him.

Then I check it again, just to be sure.

I'm not crazy . . . right?

TWELVE

Stretching, I let my eyes flutter open. Sunlight is pouring through my bedroom window, past the curtains, shining across my bed. It's warm enough to have woken me from my sleep. I must have slept in longer than I thought, because I'm usually up before the sun. Groaning, I roll my stiff body from the bed and throw my feet onto the ground, standing up. I adjust my cotton shorts and tank, moving them from the off position they crept into as I was sleeping.

Coffee.

Stat.

As I walk out into the hall and down into the kitchen, my eyes flick to the door—the locks are all in place. I exhale and move towards my coffeepot, but stop dead when I see a cup on the counter. My heart starts racing immediately, and for a moment, I just stare at it. This can't even be passed off as maybe Jacob having stopped in and left me a coffee, or Taylor, or even Ace.

Because the cup the coffee is in is the one Raymond gave me for our first wedding anniversary. It's bright pink and has big, bold writing that says YUMMY FUTURE MOMMY. We had started trying for a baby after we were married, and so he purchased it for me so I would smile every morning. It has been packed away for years. In fact, I had nearly forgotten about it.

With trembling knees, I move towards the counter and stare down at the cup, reaching out and grazing my fingers over it. It's still hot! My eyes move to the left, where a note is neatly folded beside it. No. No. No. With blurred vision and shaking fingers, I reach down and pick up the note. I know, even before I unfold it, what it'll say. It was the same thing every single morning. I kept a few of the notes, because I loved them so much.

> *My darling Hartley,*
> *A coffee to wake you, two kisses to keep you thinking of me, and three hours until I hear your sweet voice.*
> *Have a great day, my sweet.*
>
> *R xx*

I can't keep it in—a sob rises up and releases loudly from my throat. I tremble and clutch the side of the counter, scrunching the note in my hand. My sob is one of fear and sadness. I'm not crazy. I know that now. There is simply no way I would have done this. Which means someone is doing this to me. Someone is trying to get to me, using the one thing I hold dearest—my husband.

My eyes flicker around the house, and I'm suddenly filling with panic.

What if someone is in here now?

I don't think, I just turn and run to the door, tears streaming down my face as I fumble with the locks, getting them open before swinging the door open so hard it slams against the doorstop. Then I go charging out and down the hall. I reach Ace's door, and I pound. I don't know what the time is. I don't care. I simply pray he's home. I'm terrified. I can feel it right down to my bones, clutching my stomach like an iron fist.

The door swings open and Ace stands in the space, wearing a suit, his hair still wet from a shower. His eyes drop to me, then to the note in my hand, and he asks in a calm, but edgy, voice, "Hartley, what's wrong?"

"Someone is m-m-m-messing with me, Ace."

I can't even speak.

"Come here."

He takes my shoulder and pulls me into his apartment, shutting the door behind him. He guides my body towards a kitchen stool, pushing me slightly so I sit down on it. When my bottom is firmly in place, he lowers his body until we're eye level. "Look at me."

I blink a few times, trying to clear my blurred vision.

"Hart, look at me."

Hart.

Look at him.

I take a shaky breath as my eyes meet his. There is not an ounce of panic in his gaze, just calm authority. I bite my tongue to stop the next sob escaping, and just hold his eyes, not wanting for a second to look away, because he's grounding me and I'm afraid I'll lose it all over again.

"Take a few deep breaths. Breathe in as deep as you can, hold a few seconds, and let it out."

I do as he says, inhaling deeply, holding the breath in my lungs for a few seconds, and then letting it out. I do this a few times, until the sob stuck in my throat disappears and my tears stop flowing pathetically down my cheeks. Only then does Ace straighten up, grab another stool, and sit back down in front of me.

"Now, tell me what happened," he orders, probably in the kindest voice I've ever heard him use, even though it's still gruff and a little scary.

"Well." I take another deep breath. "I woke up this morning, and when I walked into the kitchen, there was a cup of already made coffee on my counter. It was still hot, too. And I know it wasn't just dropped off by Taylor or Jacob, because the cup was a gift from my husband. He used to leave me coffee in it every morning, with this note."

I hand Ace the note that's still scrunched in my hand.

He glances down at it. "This your husband's handwriting?"

"Yes, I had a few of those notes saved. He used to write the same one every morning."

Ace nods, looking back up at me. "All of the things happening, they're all in relation to your husband, and nothing else, am I correct?"

I nod, swallowing.

"Right," he murmurs, humming for a second, before standing. "I'm still waiting on those locks. They're supposed to arrive later today or at the very latest, tomorrow morning. I'll put them on, but I am still looking into things. I spoke to security—nothing out of the ordinary, but the security on this place is hardly something to cheer about."

I chew my cheek, trying to stop the fear from taking over again.

"Anyone who lives in the area that you know, be it a family member, friend, acquaintance, I want their full names. Anyone in the area your husband used to know, including any old girlfriends you may know about, I want their full names. Anyone you have had any interaction with in the last few months, I want as many details as you can provide me. Can you get me that list by this afternoon?"

I nod. "What do you think is happening?"

"There could be a few explanations and I have a few theories, but I think it's safe to say you're not doing this on your own, someone is doing it to you. What I want to know is who and why."

"Do you"—I swallow and take another deep breath—"do you think I'm in danger?"

He hesitates. "I don't honestly know at this stage. I need more information. So far, whoever is doing this hasn't hurt you or tried to hurt you at all. That's a good sign. However, figuring out why someone is choosing to leave reminders of your ex-husband lying around, obviously *trying* to freak you out, could be hard to figure out. It's not being done in secret, which means whoever it is wants you to know they're doing it."

That thought makes me want to vomit. I simply don't understand why anyone would want to do that to me, especially not so long after I lost my husband.

"I'll get a rush on these locks. The system has been down for the last few weeks but I've told them to get that fixed immediately or the landlord would be held responsible for anything that happened."

"W-W-What about my windows?" I ask, thinking of them all of a sudden. I mean, it's a possibility, right? Any entrance is access into my house.

He nods. "I'll be adding locks to those, too. If need be, I'll have the station get a watch put on the place, or we'll install an alarm system."

God. This is too much.

I press a hand to my chest and drop my head, staring at the ground and taking a few shaky breaths.

"We'll get to the bottom of this, Hartley," Ace says. "I'll make sure of it. Please trust that I'll do whatever I can to keep you safe."

Whatever he can.

Whatever. He. Can.

What if that's not enough?

"Seriously, it's creepy," Taylor mumbles, shoving her fork into a piece of curry chicken we just ordered from a local restaurant.

"I feel you." I sigh, poking my food with my fork, not sure I can actually eat any of it. My stomach has been twisting all day.

"You've given Ace your list. Did anyone raise a red flag?"

I shrug. "All of our friends, we've known forever. All of Raymond's friends, even the few ex's he had, I am familiar with them all. I hardly doubt they'd start tormenting me years after his death. The only ones I think might have even a chance at being that weird are the men I went on blind dates with."

Her eyes widen. "Oh god. I forgot about them. Oh, what if this is my fault?"

I reach over, patting her shoulder. "It isn't, honestly. I had the briefest interactions with them. They didn't even know my full name, let alone how to find me less than a month after dating them. I honestly can't see that being the case. But Ace is looking into them anyway."

"Jacob?" she questions.

I shake my head. "No, Ace did a full background check on him first. He's as clean as a whistle, not even a parking ticket. And honestly, he's been so kind to me."

Taylor rolls her eyes. "Of course he checked him out first."

I laugh softly. "Yeah, that's what I said."

"Bloody males. And you're sure it wasn't Greg or Richard?"

I nod. "Yeah. I don't think Richard has it in him, considering he was so broken up over his ex. That wasn't an act—at least, I don't think it was. And Greg, I guess out of everyone, he might be most likely, because I offended him. But I still don't think he'd go to this extreme, right?"

Taylor purses her lips in thought. "You did really upset him, though. I mean, what do we know about him? How do we know he isn't some stalker? He did lie about his profile, so maybe he felt like getting revenge?"

I contemplate this. Out of everyone, Greg is definitely the most likely to do something like this. I've given Ace his details, so I guess now I have to wait and see what he comes up with.

"Yeah, I did tell Ace about him, and he said he's going to be looking into it." Whoever has done this, has done research. How else would they know the little things?"

She nods, rubbing her chin. "Yeah, you're right. Still, people can find out any information about you if they try hard enough. I mean, it happens all the time."

"Hmmm." I ponder that, and my heart clenches at the thought. "Well, I can only hope that whoever it is, Ace will find them soon. I really, really hope he does."

She shoves another piece of chicken into her mouth. "I hope so, too. It makes me so uneasy."

I nod. "Me too. Believe me. I can't sleep now. I think I'll struggle even knowing someone is here. If we're correct, someone was in my house while I was asleep . . . walking around . . . that makes me feel sick just thinking about what they could have done if they wanted to."

Taylor reaches over, squeezing my knee. "We're going to get this sorted. Until then, I'll stay as many nights as I can, you know that. And you can stay at my house, too, if you really need to."

"You already have a roommate and no extra room. I couldn't do that. It's okay. It'll be fine, I'm sure."

A knock sounds at the door, and both our heads swivel in the general direction it came from. I shoot a look to Taylor, but she's already standing, walking over to the door and calling out, "Who is it?"

"Ace."

Gruff. Masculine. No missing that voice.

She glances over her shoulder at me, and I nod,

giving her the go-ahead to let him in. She unlocks
the door and pulls it open. Ace stands in the space,
holding a bag in his hands. His eyes flick to Taylor,
narrow for a second as he takes her in, and then
swing over to me sitting on the couch, a bowl of
untouched food in my lap.

"Hey," I say, my voice flat-sounding, even to me.

"I just wanted to check in on you before I went
home. I have a couple of things to give you, and
some information."

I nod, stretching a hand and encouraging him in.
He gives Taylor another glance and then walks
in, sitting on the chair across from me, his eyes
scanning my face.

His eyes take in all of me, but mostly they focus
on my own. I swear, it feels like he can see everything I'm trying to keep inside. Way past any wall
I've put up, and right into the most vulnerable parts.

"You good?" he murmurs, that voice low, husky
and . . . almost genuine.

"I'm doing as well as I can," I tell him, and that's
the truth.

He nods, then puts the bag down in front of me.
"It isn't much, but there are a couple of things in
there you can use if you . . . need to."

My eyes flash to Taylor's and even those words
seem to make her uncomfortable. She shifts slightly,
crossing her arms and frowning.

"Pepper spray, a whistle that'll make anyone retreat, and a list of direct emergency numbers to some
other officers at the station, including my own."

My hands start shaking, so I shove them beneath
my thighs and look over to Ace, holding his stare.
"Thank you, that makes me feel better."

It really doesn't. I honestly don't think anything could at this point, but the fact that he's thought of it does ease something inside me.

He nods briskly. "I've looked over everyone on your list, and they are all coming up clear. That's not to say they're not capable of pulling this off, but I think I'm going to start looking at outside sources, even strangers, people you work with, people who live in these apartments, things like that."

"Thank you Ace," I say genuinely. "I really appreciate it."

He shrugs. "I'd do it for anyone."

Right. That has my chest tightening, surprising me. I don't like how that felt when he said those words. I try not to think too much about why that might be.

He stands. "I'm right next door, yell out if you need me. Make sure you lock these doors, double-check them. I'll have the new locks tomorrow."

I nod, swallowing the thick lump in my throat. "Thank you."

He nods again. "Later."

He walks out of the apartment without another look back. I glance over at Taylor, who watches him go and then looks at me. "He's intense."

Yes.

Yes he is.

But he makes me feel strangely safe, and right now I'll take that.

THIRTEEN

Lightning cracks outside, lighting up my bedroom as it makes a loud crashing sound, followed by a loud boom of thunder. Heavy rain falls, causing a waterfall to run down my window. I'm on my bed, legs tucked up to my chest, with every light on, staring out at the storm currently wreaking havoc on our city.

I like storms.

Tonight, though, I'm not feeling all that great about it.

It's just past one in the morning, and I know sleep won't come to me. Especially not after Taylor got called into work. She was going to stay the night, and now she can't. I'm alone and there is no way in hell I'll be able to sleep. So, I left every light on, and decided I'd ride this night out. What's one night without sleep? Even so, the heaviness in my chest won't ease.

Not even a little.

Every single tiny sound I hear has my heart

nearly launching out of my throat. I'm terrified. I wish Raymond was here, I wish it so heavily the ache in my chest spreads, traveling up my throat until my nose tickles with unshed tears. I wish he was here, and none of this was happening. He'd know how to make me feel safe. He'd know how to make me feel better.

I'm plunged into pitch-black.

For a second, my breathing stops.

No.

God. Not again.

The power is out.

My hands start shaking and my entire body feels too heavy to move. I'm frozen in the spot, trying to force myself to get up, but nothing is happening. I'm stuck here, terrified. A loud crack of lightning lights up my room, and a scream leaves my throat. Where's my phone? Where is it? It'll have a light. God, why did I stay here? I should have thought this through. I should have gone to Taylor's house, anywhere but here.

What was I thinking?

Tears burn under my eyelids and I know I have to stand up and move. I'll go next door, Ace won't mind. Hell, I'll sleep on the floor in his apartment if I have to. I don't care if he doesn't like me. I can't stay here. With shaky fingers, I remember my phone is on the bedside table, so I reach over to get it and flick it on. Just as I go to turn the built-in flashlight on, it rings.

It. Rings.

And Raymond's name flashes up on the screen.

No.

A terrified gurgle escapes my throat and I launch

the phone across the room, stumbling out of the bed. My eyes dart to the left, then to the right, then to the open door in front of me. Did I leave that open? God. I didn't. I'm sure I closed it when I went to bed. I'm sure of it. A sound travels out from the kitchen. Was that lightning? Is someone in my house? Panic grips my chest and I can't breathe. I can't breathe.

"Help," I croak as my phone starts ringing somewhere in the room again.

Who is doing this to me?

Why?

My knees wobble. I can't see anything. The only time I can see even briefly is when the lightning comes again, hitting the ground outside and sparking up the room for a flash of a second. My hand darts out to my left, trying to find a wall to hang onto. I need to get to my phone. Ace's number is on there. I'll call him. Everything will be okay. It'll all be okay.

That's it.

That's all I have to do.

It feels like two hands are squeezing my windpipe, I'm so afraid. A cold sweat breaks out on my forehead and I can't seem to get it together. Not even enough to think. A crashing sound comes from my general kitchen area, and my blood runs cold. Someone is in my house? Oh God, someone is in my house! With trembling hands, I try to remember where I put the bag Ace gave me. It's on the desk, right near my bed. It's there, I need to get to it.

My phone first. Call Ace. Get it together.

Lightning hits, and my eyes are trained on my

open bedroom door. The room lights up, and in the doorframe I see a dark, hooded figure. I scream, I scream so loud my voice cuts off midway through and nothing further comes out. My knees give way and I drop to the ground, jerking my head back up when another bolt of lightning hits.

This time there is no one in the doorway.

"Ace!" I screech as loudly as I can. I don't know if he can hear me. I don't know anything, but I just keep screaming his name over and over until my voice cracks and I back myself up so I'm pressed against my bedframe. I stay curled there, eyes on the door, terrified.

Someone is in my house.

I saw him with my own eyes.

I can't move. I need to find my phone, I know that, but the fear is holding me hostage. I can't move.

"Help," I sob, bringing my knees up to my chest. "Please."

There is a crashing sound, then a pounding at my front door. "Hartley?"

Ace.

He heard me.

"Hartley?"

He's yelling, and I can hear his voice as clear as day.

"Door is locked. Hartley."

The door is locked? But . . . but someone was in my house. I saw him. I . . . I did. I saw him. Am I going crazy? Am I losing my mind? What the hell is happening? I fall forward so I'm on my hands and knees and I crawl towards the bedroom door, croaking out, "Ace?"

"Open the door for me," he yells.

He's right there. No one will hurt me if he's right there.

Taking a deep, staggering breath, I push to my feet and I run, I run towards the front door with all my might. With shaky fingers, I fumble around with the locks in the dark until they spring open. Then I step back, sinking to my knees, my body too full of fear to function. I know there are tears streaming down my face, even though I can't really feel them.

A flashlight swings around the room, before settling on me.

"Shit."

The muttered curse is followed by two big arms circling me, and lifting me into the air as if I weigh nothing. I curl my fingers into Ace's shirt and I latch on. I don't care that he's basically a perfect stranger, and one who doesn't like me most of the time, all I care about is that the comfort he brings me in that moment is overwhelming.

Ace moves to the sofa, lowering himself until he's sitting. There is no way I'm letting him go anytime soon—he can hate it as much as he likes. I'm so damned afraid, I need something to cling on to and he's going to be that person, whether he likes it or not. He is seemingly okay with my grabbing him like I need him to breathe, though I can feel the tightness of his muscles where they press against my body.

He doesn't do this often, that much is obvious, but he's doing it for me and I'm grateful.

"Calm down," he says, his voice tight, like he really has no idea what he's supposed to be doing. He stares into my eyes, and he holds them, bringing a calm over me that I honestly wouldn't think possible right now. "You're barely breathing, Hartley. Practice what I showed you—into your lungs, hold it, let it out."

I do as he asks, sucking air into my sore lungs, and holding it for a few seconds before I let it back out again. I do this for a solid ten minutes before my body finally starts feeling like my own again. My legs stop being numb, my hands stop trembling, and I manage to pry myself from Ace with a flush on my cheeks. I slide off his lap and into the spot directly beside him.

The power flicks back on, and I shield my eyes as the light feels that much brighter now that it's been out for a while. I rub my eyes a few times, and then blink rapidly when I uncover them to get them adjusted. When I glance over at Ace, he's staring at me, and his eyes search over me, starting on my face and traveling over my body. Is he looking to see if I'm injured? Did he think I was hurt?

"What happened?" he asks.

I swallow and rub my upper arms. I'm cold even though it really isn't cool in here at all.

"I heard some noises," I say softly. "And my phone rang. My husband's phone was calling. Then, I swear Ace, I saw someone in my doorway. A man, I think, wearing a black hoodie. I could be wrong, because when the lightning lit up the room again, there was nobody there. And then when you came over, the door was locked . . ."

Ace stands. "Where's your phone?"

"I threw it in the bedroom."

"Wait here."

He disappears down the hall in a few long strides.

He's gone for a few minutes before reappearing again with my phone in his hand. He's staring down at the screen. "There are some missed calls from your husband's number. I don't think you were imagining it."

"I know I wasn't imagining that," I say, tucking my knees up to my chest. "But do you think someone was in here?"

He walks off again, and is gone for another few minutes, searching through the apartment before returning and standing in front of me, looking down. "There doesn't seem to be any sign of forced entry."

My heart plummets. So am I losing it then? Was I seeing things? God, I could swear someone was standing in my doorway. I could swear it as surely as I breathe.

Ace must see the expression on my face, because he says carefully, "That's not to say you didn't see someone, it's just however they got in, they're a pro at it."

I feel like he's just trying to make me feel better now.

"Ace?" I ask, looking up.

"Mmmm?"

"Do you think I'm crazy?"

His brows knit together, and he says in a low, gruff tone, "Absolutely fucking not."

I don't know why, but that makes me start crying again. Big ugly tears roll down my cheeks and I feel stupid for being so weak. My mind is a jumbled mess, and I'm tired, and I'm trying to make sense of everything. Ace is silent for a moment, so long I wonder if he's still in the room, but then he squats down in front of me and surprises me by taking my chin in his hands, forcing my head up just enough so that he can make eye contact with me.

"This is a lot to take in and I know you're probably questioning everything right now, but don't question yourself. You're not crazy. You're being messed with, and I'm goin' to find who is messin' with you, and make them fuckin' stop. Do you understand me?"

My bottom lip quivers.

"I'm the best in my field, Hartley. Now, I ask again, do you understand me?"

"Yes," I whisper.

"Good. How do you take your tea? I'm going to make you one and then you're going to get some sleep."

It isn't a question, but a demand.

And I don't argue it.

Having him here makes me feel safe, so there is no way I'll continue to argue with anything he's willing to give me.

I need him here.

"How did you lose your husband?" Ace asks, sitting at one end of the sofa. I'm tucked up the other end with a blanket wrapped around the lower half of my body and a cup of tea resting between my hands.

"He died in a car accident," I tell him, and I realize it's been a long time since I've really told anyone about Raymond. "It's the age-old story, really. He was driving home and it was raining, a car lost control and ran him off the road. His truck flipped and he was killed instantly."

Ace studies me. "I'm sorry. It's never easy to lose someone you love."

He sounds like he knows.

"No, it wasn't easy. I struggled for a long time. I loved him, wholeheartedly. He was a great man, the best. He was the kind of husband you read about, the kind everyone envied. It felt like a cruel twist of fate, that something would come along and rip it from me so easily."

He nods. "He sounds like a good man."

"He was." I nod. Talking about him out loud feels good. "What about you?" I ask him before sipping my tea. "Have you ever been married?"

His eyes flash, and he looks to me. "Yeah."

Oh.

Oh my.

There is something in his eyes. I can see it so clearly, because I've seen it in my own eyes thousands of times in the last four years when I have looked in the mirror. It's an emptiness, a sadness most would overlook. But I can see it so clearly. He's been hurt. In a big way.

So I ask in a soft tone, "Is your wife still around?"

Pain flashes across those depths, before he roughly shakes his head. "No. She passed away. Breast cancer."

So he does know how it feels, I was right. He does understand the pain I felt. The kind of pain no words in the world could ever describe. The kind of pain that rips into your soul, and lodges itself there, until nothing you can do will remove it. It hangs around like a constant ache, a growth you can't remove. Even on your best days, you can feel it, just thrumming away, reminding you of what you lost.

"I'm so sorry, Ace," I whisper, and my voice is soft and genuine. "I know exactly how much it hurts."

"Yeah," he mutters gruffly. "I know you do."

"Was it long ago?"

"Two years."

Poor guy. Two years, in the grand scheme of things, seems like a long time, but when you lose someone you love, it passes in the blink of an eye and you feel like nothing has changed, like nothing is moving forward, like you'll never be okay again.

"I'm really sorry," I say again, because, what else is there to say?

There's a long pause before he asks, "You ever want any kids?"

"Yeah," I answer him. "We tried, but he passed before we could ever make too much of an effort. Did you?"

He shakes his head.

Right.

It's clear this conversation has come to an end for now. He's obviously not wanting to talk about it, so I decide to change the subject and put him out of his misery.

"How long have you been a detective?"

That's always a safe subject. Talking about someone's work.

"Seven years, but I was a cop for three years before that."

"Do you like it?" I ask, rubbing my hands around the mug, warming them up.

He nods. "It's demanding, but I like the challenge it presents."

"I can only imagine. I don't know how you do it. The kind of mind you must have, to be able to go through all those clues and figure out a crime, it's pretty impressive."

"Yeah, it keeps me busy."

I can imagine. I nod and give him a small smile. "I bet."

"What about you? Why did you decide to become a midwife?"

I meet his eyes. Of course he knows what I'm studying, I forgot he did a background check on me. "I love kids. I love babies. I just love the idea of helping bring life into the world. I thought about studying to be an OB, but decided a midwife was what I wanted to do."

Ace stares at me, and doesn't say anything, he just studies me.

"You're an incredibly intense man, has anyone ever told you that?"

He grunts. "Yeah. Often."

"I think if you let that guard down a little, there might just be a lot of good beneath the surface."

He keeps studying me, his lip twitches slightly, and it's like he can't make sense of something, or maybe he's trying to figure something out.

"You like that dick you're seeing?"

I blink.

Random change of subject.

"Jacob?"

He nods.

"Yeah," I say. "I mean, we're just casually dating and seeing if there is a future to proceed onto. He's a nice guy."

Ace snorts. "He's a wimp."

I hold back my grunt, and maybe a little giggle.

"He's not a wimp. He's really kind."

"And a wimp."

"You're being a little nasty again," I point out, raising my brows.

He grunts. "How is being honest considered being nasty?"

I contemplate this. "I don't think it's so much that you're trying to be nasty, but the way you word things can come across as . . . cold."

He raises a brow.

"It's true," I point out. "You don't know Jacob. So it's a little far-fetched for you to call him a wimp . . . don't you think?"

He shakes his head. "No, I don't think that. I call it like it see it, with everyone I meet. I deal with people all the time, and I know the weak ones, the ones who go running when shit gets hard. That man couldn't defend you if he tried. He's like all those other men out there, who sit back and do nothing when their women need them."

"What about me?" I say, my voice going a little softer. "Call it like you see it . . ."

He studies me a moment, and I think he's not going to answer, but in a throaty voice he says, "You use your sarcasm and quick wit to avoid your feelings. You're scared, maybe of moving on, maybe of living, maybe of getting hurt. I'm not sure. You're softer than you come across, but you're also incredibly strong. Those who have lived through what you have are, by far, some of the strongest people you'll ever meet. You don't give yourself enough credit for that, and you should."

My heart flutters, and for a moment I just stare at him, holding those intense eyes.

God.

He's doing strange things to my heart, he's cracking open a wall I've built up so high. I look away quickly.

"Time for sleep," Ace says, his voice low, but kind. "You look exhausted."

"I don't . . . I don't . . ." I glance down the hall at my room.

I don't know if I have it in me to sleep in there. What if someone comes through the window while Ace is sleeping out here . . . or . . .

"Ace?"

He glances at me, midway through reaching for a pillow. "Yeah?"

"Can we go and sleep at your place?"

He studies me, and for a second he looks horrified at the thought. Like it terrifies him to no end. I'm already opening my mouth to tell him not to worry when he throws out a gruff, "Yeah."

Thank God.

Oh. Thank. God.

FOURTEEN

I wake up, my back on what is probably the comfiest couch I've ever slept on. I blink my eyes open, and it takes a moment to remember where I am. Ace's apartment. I swing my eyes around the room, getting the blurriness from them, and take in the space. Sleek, modern, and clean. Ace has good taste. Everything is either black, gray, or red. His furniture is masculine.

The whole apartment is masculine.

My eyes move to the kitchen, which is in the exact same place as mine. The apartments are laid out identically. Ace is standing at the counter, tapping away at his open laptop. He hasn't realized I'm awake. My cheeks flush. I barely know him, and here I am sleeping on his couch. Did I snore? God, did I lay there with my mouth wide open. Worse, did I drool?

Oh god, what if I drooled?

And he saw.

I raise a hand and run it through my messy hair,

catching his attention. His eyes flick to me, and something twists inside my chest. It isn't an unpleasant feeling, in fact, it's a feeling I'm not overly familiar with. It feels warm, safe even. I squash it back down and mumble a sleepy, "Hi."

He nods. "Morning."

"What time is it?"

"Eight."

I thought I might have slept longer than that, but I'm glad I didn't. I sit up, adjusting my clothes and making sure they're all in the right place, before sliding off the couch. I fold the blanket and place it on the end, and then stack the pillows on top before walking towards the counter. Ace slides a coffee towards me without looking up.

My heart warms.

He made me coffee.

"Thank you," I say, taking it in my hands.

"I'm going to take a few things from your apartment into the station today, check to see if I can get any fingerprints, anything like that. The locks have arrived. I'll put them on before lunch and you should be safe to go home then."

I swallow.

Even though he says that, the idea of going home terrifies me. That whole apartment feels unsafe now.

"I'm going to run a few more checks, see what I can figure out. I'd like you to stay here, at least until I change the locks. Can you study here?"

He wants me to stay . . . here? At his house?

"Ah, yeah, I can grab my laptop and study from here. I have to work tonight, is that going to be a problem?"

He shakes his head. "I'll drop you off, so I know

you get there safe. Pick you back up when you're done."

"Is it normal for, ah, detectives to do all of that?"

He finally looks back up at me. "I'm not your detective when I'm here, Hartley. I'm your neighbor. And yes, it is normal."

Right.

Still, I have never heard of any police officer or detective going to such extremes to help someone. Usually they give the job of watching a person in danger to one of the rookies, and go about their business. It warms my heart that Ace is wanting to help me out, on his own personal watch. That means a lot to me. I should probably allow Jacob to do it, but I'm still not ready to let him do that yet, still not ready for that kind of change in our relationship. Besides, Ace is a cop . . . it makes more sense.

"Okay." I nod in agreement. "Whatever is easiest."

"Hopefully I'll get some sort of lead in the next few days, to try to figure out what it is we're working with here."

My phone rings, and I glance around, wondering where it is. Ace had it last night, and obviously brought it over here. He glances down, and I see it's sitting beside his laptop. Making a cranky face, he picks it up and answers it.

He answers my phone.

My mouth drops open when he mutters a grumbled, "Jacob."

Oh.

Boy.

"She's at my house, under my protection at this stage. Until I can clear you, I'll need you to keep your distance."

My heart slams against my ribcage, because I know he's already cleared Jacob. I know he has, because he told me. So why is he telling him that he hasn't?

"She's fine. She had a scare last night."

Ace looks up to the ceiling.

Impatient.

"Five minutes."

He hangs up and slams the phone down, focusing back on the laptop.

"Uh," I begin. "What was that?"

"He'll be here soon. I told him he can have five minutes."

"You answered my phone."

He looks up. "So?"

"So . . . it's my phone."

"Yeah, and you're under my care right now."

"Actually, I'm not—"

He shoots me a look that has me backing down right away. "You're being harassed, you're my neighbor, you stayed at my house, and I'm investigating your case. Right now, you're my business. I'd rather you didn't get murdered right next door to me. So stop arguing with me and do as you're told."

Oh.

My.

God.

"Ace," I growl. "Jacob is my business, and that is my phone."

He ignores me.

"You have no right to speak to someone who is important to me like that."

He keeps ignoring me.

"I'm speaking to you!" I snap.

He glances at me again. "I'm keeping you safe, Hartley."

"No," I growl, frustrated. "You're acting like a jealous, overprotective boyfriend right now. That isn't protection. You could have spoken kindly to him, or let me answer the phone with you nearby. Instead you took the jerk route . . ."

He makes an angry sound in his throat. "Be careful."

I shake my head. "You're out of line."

He narrows his eyes and we glare at each other for what feels like a solid minute, neither of us breaking. I'm angry, and I have the right to be. A knock at the door distracts me from wanting to throttle Ace, and I walk over to it, swinging it open to see Jacob standing outside. The second he sees me, he steps forward and wraps me in a giant hug. "Are you okay?"

I let my arms fall around his waist, and I glance over at Ace, who is glaring at us, mostly me.

"I'm okay. I just had a bit of a long night."

Jacob pulls back and looks down at me, and I adjust the casual white halter dress I'm wearing to make sure it hasn't ridden up. "You look exhausted. What happened?"

"That's police business," Ace says from his corner in the kitchen, not saying hello or even trying to use manners.

Jacob scowls at him, before looking back down at me. "Can you at least tell me if you're safe?"

"I'm . . . safe as I can be," I answer.

"I don't like this, Hartley. I don't like being kept in the dark about your safety."

Okay.

This is a little intense, considering the man and I barely know each other. I do feel a little guilty though. I haven't spent a good deal of time with Jacob, and I haven't actually thought a great deal about him when we aren't together. I know, deep down in my heart, that my emotions aren't truly there for him. Granted, I'm hardly making a big effort, but when I'm with Ace, I feel it, right down to my toes. I don't feel that with Jacob. Will that come? Is it just because I'm not getting enough time to truly know him?

I'm not sure. It's a little confusing.

"Not your concern, I've got her covered," Ace throws in again before I even get the chance to answer Jacob.

Gosh.

This is getting weird. Anyone would think it's a competition between the two men, but that isn't the case, since Ace barely likes me.

"I'm sorry, I wish I could tell you more but I can't," I say to Jacob.

"You should have called and told me something was wrong."

I give him a "whoopsie" expression, and chew on my bottom lip for a moment before answering with, "Sorry. I've just been really stressed."

What a terrible, terrible answer.

Even I wouldn't believe it.

It sounds like I'm palming him off. Hell, maybe I am.

I don't know.

"I understand," he sighs, eyes flicking to Ace again before coming back to me. "Please at least keep me updated. I'm worried."

I nod. "Of course, thanks for checking in on me."

He leans down, pressing a kiss to my forehead. "I have to get to work. Call me later, okay?"

"Okay."

He gives Ace one more look, then disappears out the door. I turn, and Ace is already opening his mouth. I put up one finger and mutter, "Don't even start."

He closes his mouth.

Smart man.

FIFTEEN

Stretching, I walk out of the hospital where I just did an eight-hour training shift with some senior midwives. I'm exhausted, after such a short time, and I know it'll take years to build up the stamina some of those older ladies have. It's incredible how they can work around the clock, on their feet all day, using their hands constantly. I take my hat off to them, it can't be easy.

I walk out the front doors and turn left, making my way towards the parking lot a few blocks down where I'm parked. I don't use my old car a great deal, because I'm so close to everything and finding a parking spot can be difficult at times, but Ace prefers me to drive instead of using public transportation at this time so I agreed. I'm looking forward to going home and getting a good night's sleep. I haven't slept for the past week and even though Ace has put new locks on, and I've had no more strange occurrences since, I still don't feel at ease. I still find it hard to settle in at night.

Ace thinks it's a good sign nothing more has happened since the locks have been changed, but I still don't feel right. I always feel as though someone is watching me. Jacob told me I'm imagining it, and that it's probably just leftover paranoia from the scare I had, but I just can't shake the feeling that it's more than that. It doesn't matter how hard I try to rationalize it in my head, I don't feel any better.

It's been raining again tonight, and the sidewalk is slippery as I walk down towards the parking lot. I reach it and am just moving around to the driver's door of my car when I step in something that looks a little like oil. I slip right away, hands going out to try to stop myself. I miss and come crashing down onto the hard ground, my ankle twisting angrily beneath me.

I cry out as a sharp pain shoots up my leg.

Dammit.

That was bad.

Wincing, I roll to my butt and look down at my ankle. It's throbbing already, and I can see the swelling rising. That was a good twist, good enough that my stomach twists too as the pain starts getting more intense with every passing second. I bite my bottom lip to stop myself from crying and try to move my ankle, to see if I can stand. Sharp pain hits me hard, and I know I can't stand on it.

Honestly. Why?

I reach into my purse, which is now soaked from having landed on the ground, and I pull out my phone, glancing down at the screen. Should I dial Jacob? Yeah, I probably should. I can't ring the hospital and ask someone to walk two blocks to get me, that would make things even more embarrassing. Sighing, I hit his number and bring the phone to my ear, trying to stop myself from sobbing hysterically when he answers, because the pain in my foot is out of this world.

"Hey, sweetheart."

"Jacob," I croak. "Are you still in the city by any chance?"

"Yeah," he answers, his voice growing concerned. "What's the matter?"

"I slipped over at my car, near the hospital. I don't think I can stand up, and I don't really want to call a staff member out to help me."

"Of course. I'm probably only five minutes away from the hospital. Are you okay? Where you are?"

I wince as I try to shift so my back is pressed against the car door. "Yeah, I'm in the parking lot. Unless a mugger comes in the next five minutes, I think I'm safe."

I try to joke, but it's really a pathetic attempt. Even I don't laugh.

"Sit tight, I'm on my way."

He hangs up and I glance at the screen of the phone, noticing a couple of messages I must have missed earlier. Both are from Ace. I saved his number into my phone a few days ago, and he keeps me updated as much as possible, letting me know if he finds anything, or when he questions someone.

A: Is everything okay?

I narrow my eyes at the message. He never asks if anything is okay. Sure, he checks in on me when he comes home from work each night, but he doesn't send it over text, and he never calls. I wonder why he's asking.

H: I'm ok. I slipped outside the hospital, so I'm
   going to get my ankle looked at and then
   I'll head home.

My phone rings a few minutes later, Ace's name flashing on the screen.

"Ah, hello?" I answer, more than a little confused.

"You okay?" Ace's demanding voice comes across
the phone speaker.

"Yes, I just hurt my ankle."

"Where are you?"

Um. Bossy.

"In the hospital parking lot. I'm waiting for Jacob to show up and help me back into the hospital
to get it looked at."

"How did you slip?"

"Ace," I say, wincing as I shift. "You're starting
to freak me out."

"I need to talk to you. Text me as soon as you
know what's happening, or when you're at home.
I'll come to you."

My heart twists.

That doesn't make me feel good . . . at all.

"Ace," I say again, my voice weary. "What's
going on?"

"Are you alone in that parking lot?"

Suddenly I feel unsafe. My eyes scan around and
thus far, I can't see anything or anyone. My heart
pounds against my ribcage, and I don't feel okay,
at all. The pain in my ankle gets seemingly worse
when I think about the fact that I can't run, even if
I need to.

"You're scaring me," I whisper.

"Keep me on the phone until Jacob gets there."

"Ace, seriously, what's going on?"

"I'm not going to discuss it over the phone."

His voice is gruff, and straight down the line, leaving no room for argument.

"Am I . . . in danger?"

"I don't know, but we need to talk. Is he there yet?"

God.

I don't feel so good.

"Not yet."

"How did you slip?"

I glance at the oil-like substance I'm now sitting in. "I think maybe my car is leaking, or someone else's car, there is something that resembles oil on the ground."

Ace goes quiet for a minute. "Is it by any other cars?"

I wasn't paying that much attention. I look over at the other empty parking spots, and they're all wet from the rain, but none of them seem to have the shine coating them like the spot I'm in does. Great. Just what I need, a leaking damned car to fix.

"No," I finally answer Ace. "I think my car is leaking."

He doesn't say anything, he just makes a strange sound in his throat.

"Hart?"

Jacob's voice calls out, and I yell back, "I'm here."

Then I focus back on the phone. "Jacob is here now."

"Text me when you get into the hospital, and if they send you home, let me know."

My heart squeezes with dread again. "Okay Ace."

"Later."

He hangs up and I stare at my phone in confusion, then I lift my head just in time to see Jacob rounding my car. He takes one look at me and his face goes soft. He walks over, avoiding the spill, and squats down, glancing at my ankle. "That's swollen, Hartley. Are you in pain?"

I nod. "Yeah, it hurts a lot."

"I'm going to lift you up and take you into the hospital. Are you ready?"

I give him a weak thumbs-up and he leans down, scoops me into his arms, and lifts me up. I circle an arm around his neck as he carefully walks me across the road and into the hospital. He strolls straight up to the reception desk, and the pretty blonde who I waved good bye to only half an hour before, looks up and her eyes widen.

"What's happened?" she asks.

"I slipped and hurt my ankle. I just wanted to get it looked at," I inform her.

"It's really swollen," Jacob adds.

"Okay, head on into the ER and I'll call the nurses there and tell them you're coming."

Jacob walks me down the halls and I point him in the direction of the ER. When we get in, we explain again what is wrong and a nurse guides us to a free bed while we wait for a doctor. By now my ankle is three times its usual size and turning an ugly shade of purple. Jacob goes in search of an ice pack, and I pull out my phone to inform Ace that I'm still here.

H: I'll be at the hospital a while. It's busy tonight.

He responds a minute later.

A: I'll be there soon.

I blink. He'll what?

That doesn't make me feel good. It lodges an uneasy feeling in my belly. Ace wouldn't come here if
he didn't have good reason to, and I'm not sure I
want to know what that reason is.

At all.

SIXTEEN

Jacob has to leave after waiting with me for an hour. He said he has a late client, and can't hang around even though he'd love to. I thank him for coming for me and assure him I'm fine and that I'll call him later. Ace still hasn't arrived, but it's possible I've got another two- to three-hour wait before I get seen, considering how busy it is. Not to mention, they'll probably do X-rays, adding to the time.

So I get comfortable on the bed.

I'm tired. My eyes are heavy. The ice on my ankle has numbed some of the pain, and a nurse gave me some painkillers to help get me through until a doctor can have a look at it. That combination has helped enough to stop the sharp ache, but unfortunately, it also made me drowsy. I'm slowly starting to nod off when the curtain to my bed opens, and Ace steps in.

He looks incredible, as always, in a pair of suit pants that he has a white shirt tucked into. The sleeves are rolled up to his elbows and the top two

buttons are casually undone. His hair is poking out
in all different directions, in that messy hot way. He
looks like a businessman. The rogue kind. The kind
who will throw you over a desk and spank you with
his belt.

What the hell? It must be the meds.

I shake my head, and raise a hand. "Hey."

His eyes find mine, and narrow. Intense. So intense.

"How's your ankle?"

He reaches down before I get the chance to answer, and pulls the ice pack away from it, studying
it. My mouth drops open when he lifts it carefully
into his hands and starts inspecting it, rotating my
foot slightly. His rough calloused fingers glide over
my skin. I wince but don't jerk my foot back, instead I let him continue with his inspection. When
he's satisfied, he places it back down.

My heart is pounding.

"It's not broken," he informs me. "But it is
severely sprained. You'll be off that for at least a
week."

I blink at him. "You're a doctor too?"

He gives me an expression that has me close my
mouth instantly. "I just know basics, and I'm telling you, it's not broken."

"I'm seeing the doctor anyway."

"Wasn't sayin' you shouldn't," he mumbles.
"Where's Jacob?"

"He had to leave."

He shakes his head in disgust, but I choose to
ignore that and instead say, "Are you going to tell
me why you're here? We both know it isn't out of
genuine concern for my sore ankle."

He raises a brow, gives me a skeptical look, and then goes and sits down on the chair by the bed. "I'm not that much of a bastard," he murmurs, eyes scanning briefly over my lips before moving back to my eyes.

God.

I feel that stare deep, deep inside. It sparks something in me. Something that has been long dormant.

Lust.

Great, I'm developing a little crush on the detective.

Guilt swarms me. Poor Jacob. I like him, I really do, but I'm starting to think he just isn't my type. I mean, he certainly doesn't make me all hot under the collar the way Ace does. Not that there will ever be anything between Ace and me, but he has made me realize that I'm missing a certain spark with Jacob. I don't want to hurt him. I make a mental note to speak with him later.

"Skipping over the bastard part," I say to Ace, getting back on track. "Are you going to tell me why you're here?"

He nods, placing his elbows on his knees.

"I could be wrong about this, so don't freak out on me."

Great.

I'm freaking out just from those words.

"I've been looking over your case, really thinking about it, and it seemed familiar to me. I couldn't put my finger on why, until someone in the station mentioned something and it clicked. It's not my case, but we've all heard details about it. I don't know why I didn't consider it earlier. Probably because I wasn't directly involved."

I swallow. "And what was that case?"

His eyes hold mine. "The Bowtie Killer."

My blood runs cold.

For a second, all I can hear is my ears ringing.

I can't feel anything.

"Hartley, breathe," Ace says, but his voice sounds garbled.

Serial killer.

Serial. Killer.

No.

No he's wrong.

But I think about the new reports I read on it, and all the things that they thought happened to the other girls, and it makes sense. It does, even though I don't want to believe it. Why didn't I think of that earlier? Probably because nobody would ever believe something like that would actually happen to them. God. I feel sick.

"Hartley!"

Ace's big hand curling around my arm and shaking me a little has my eyes snapping back and focusing on his. "A-A-Are you trying to tell me you think it's the Bowtie Killer, and I'm his next . . . victim?"

Ace's face tightens. "I'm saying it's similar. The last girl had a very similar experience from what I can gather. She had lost a loved one, and things were showing up. She was tormented for months before he finally took her. We're still not sure what happens when he actually takes them, whether he continues to torment, but it is all very familiar to what's happening with you."

No.

I'm going to be sick.

"I think I'm going to throw up," I groan, clutching my stomach.

"You're not going to throw up. Breathe, Hartley."

I take a staggering breath, sweat breaks out across my forehead, and my mind is spinning. This can't be happening. He must have it wrong. It's just similar. It isn't the same. No. No. It isn't the same.

"Listen to me," Ace says, reaching up and taking my jaw, forcing me to look at him. "I could be wrong, but if I'm not, you're in the best hands. Nobody knew a thing with the other victims—he tormented them for months and nobody figured it out. We're aware of it with you. That means it's entirely different."

"How?" I croak.

"Because we can protect you."

"Nobody can be with someone twenty-four seven," I say, my voice high-pitched and worried.

"Hartley, we have many ways of protecting someone. If we're right, we'll ensure your safety."

That doesn't make me feel better.

"W-W-Why me?"

Ace studies me. "We'll discuss this later. For now, you need to calm down for me, okay?"

"Is he going to t-t-take me?" I croak, and then clutch my chest.

Ace's eyes hold mine firmly. "Not with me around, he isn't."

Why doesn't that make me feel any better?

"I've threatened the landlord with legal action if the security isn't fully updated in the apartment building. He has agreed, and some new systems should be up and running within a few days," Ace says, arm wrapped around my waist as he helps me towards my front door.

My ankle is wrapped and the doctor gave me a prescription for some good painkillers. Ace was right, it isn't broken, just badly sprained.

"I still don't really feel safe," I whisper, my body numb from exhaustion and fear.

"I've also put a watch on the building—when I'm not there, someone will be outside. Until we can find out for sure what's going on, I've got the highest security. We'll keep you safe, Hartley."

I don't know that I believe him.

"Fuck."

I blink at the random curse, and then my eyes swing up to Ace, but he's looking ahead of us. I follow his line of sight, to where he's looking, and see a massive bouquet of flowers sitting by my front door. My heart starts hammering against my rib cage, because outside of Ace and Jacob, who knew I was at the hospital?

Maybe they're from Jacob.

Yes. Yes. That makes sense.

"They're probably from Jacob," I say, but my voice is strained with anxiety.

"Probably," Ace says. "But I need to check first."

He slides his arm from around my waist and carefully presses my back against the wall before letting me go. "Stand here. Better for me to check them and make sure they're safe. It's probably nothing. I just have to be sure."

My heart feels as though it's sitting in my throat the entire time as I watch Ace move towards the flowers sitting outside my apartment in the hall, resting against the door. He kneels down, tilting his head and pressing his ear close. Is he . . . is he listening for a bomb? My knees start shaking, and I press a hand to my chest, trying to calm myself down. For a few minutes, Ace sits like that, and then he finally lifts his head back up and carefully scans the flowers.

He comes up with a card in his fingers, and quickly pulls it from the envelope and reads it.

I know the flowers aren't from Jacob when a curse floats down the hall towards me. Ace shoves the card into his pocket and continues to inspect the flowers, moving them aside, sticking his hand into the middle of them, and then finally he picks them up, strides straight past me to the end of the hall, and dumps them in the bins there.

"Ace?" I whisper when he arrives beside me again.

He doesn't say anything, he just tucks his arm back around my waist and pulls me into him again.

"Ace," I say again. "What did the card say?"

He keeps his eyes averted straight ahead, but I see the muscle in his jaw jump slightly.

This isn't good.

"Ace, please," I whisper.

He exhales, another curse passing his lips, and he looks down at me. "It said 'Take it easy on that ankle, you're so incredibly clumsy! Love you, Ray.'"

I make a pained, terrified sound in my throat, and Ace's fingers squeeze around my waist, reassuring me or just stopping me from falling, I don't know.

"Oh God, I twisted my ankle once cleaning the house, and Raymond sent me flowers with that exact card."

God.

How does this person know everything? How?

"It's okay, Hart," he murmurs, his voice distracted. "We'll figure this out."

Will we though?

"Why is he pretending to be my husband, when I already know it's not him?"

Ace unlocks my front door with the new key. "Just messing with your head, possibly trying to get you to figure out how he knows all this stuff. It's all a game."

"Why me, Ace?"

"I don't know, but I will figure it out."

He steps into my apartment and walks me over to the couch, setting me down carefully before turning and striding back to the door, locking it. He glances around for a few minutes, and then disappears down the halls. He's gone for a few more before he comes back. "There is no one in here."

I swallow. I really don't feel so good.

"Your friend Taylor, is she busy tonight?"

I nod. "She's working."

"You got any family nearby?"

I shake my head. "No, it's just me."

He nods. "Then I'll be staying again. I'll bring my work over, I have a lot to do."

It's not a question. It's just a statement.

One I don't argue with. If he wants to stay, I'm not going to try and stop him. I need someone here, because the uneasiness in my chest is getting heavier and heavier by the second. I don't want to be alone, and I certainly don't want to be left to think about the fact that I might be the next victim of a serial killer.

It just doesn't make sense.

It's something you read about in books, or see in movies, but it's not something you actually expect to happen to you. It's almost unrealistic, like it's fictional, except I know it isn't. I can feel it lodged in my chest, a fear that I'm not familiar with. I don't feel okay, I don't feel okay at all. So I won't be telling Ace he can't stay. He can stay with me every second if it means I'm not left alone.

"We're going to figure this out."

My eyes swing to his, and he's studying me. He must be reading the look of terror on my face, because he's giving me what is probably the softest expression he's ever given me.

"What if we don't?" I say, my voice a little stronger, but still shaky.

"Hartley, we will."

The thought of what will happen if the killer gets hold of me has a frightened sound rising up and escaping my lips. I press a hand over my mouth to hold it back, but Ace has already heard it and his eyes are focused on me, intense.

"Look at me."

I shake my head, squeezing my eyes shut and holding a hand firmly to my mouth to stop the noises from escaping. A big hand curls around my knee, squeezing.

"Look at me, Hartley."

I shake my head again.

That hand glides up my to my arm, pulling my hand from my mouth.

"Eyes, this way," Ace orders, his voice firm but kind.

I let my eyes focus on his, and another frightened mewl leaves my throat.

"I will not let anyone hurt you, do you understand me?"

I take a deep staggering breath. I believe him. I do.

"Do you understand me, Hartley?"

I nod. "I understand."

"Trust me."

I do.

I do trust him.

It'll be okay.

Right?

SEVENTEEN

"These are the facts," Ace says later that night, as we both sit on my couch eating takeout. I'm calmer now. He has that effect on me. He can calm me, even when I don't think it's possible. I think it's because he never freaks out, he's always calm and collected. I texted Jacob earlier, just letting him know I'm okay. I feel bad for being so distant. "First, we're assuming it's a man, due to the effortless way the women were handled. No woman could do what he did without there being signs of a struggle, not to mention another woman could fight off someone her own size."

"OK," I whisper.

Ace goes on. "I'm trying to find a link between the victims, something that helps me define his type. The only thing I know about him right now is that he must study his victims to learn everything about them. Their routine, their family, their friends. Their biggest fears. He likes to weaken them before he takes them, hence the need to torment them, which in all their cases has been the loss of a loved one."

My chest tightens, but I keep it together. I have to focus. Listen.

"What happens after he takes them?"

Ace's eyes dart away for a split second, before he looks back at me. "I'm not entirely sure—he had the last one for a little while. She was missing, the officers on the case didn't put two and two together until it was too late. When they found her, she was killed in a very specific manner. He slit her throat in a bowtie shape, carving into the skin, and then he tied an actual bowtie around her neck, but other than the gruesome manner in which she was murdered, she was seemingly unharmed. She was healthy, had clearly been taken care of."

Taken care of?

God.

"Which makes me think he mentally torments them, not physically, and then when he's broken them and had his fun, he kills them."

Oh. Lord.

"As I said, I'm not sure we're dealing with the same thing, but some of the things that have happened to you match up to what happened to the last few victims."

I take a deep breath. I can do this. I've got this. "So how do we figure out a connection?"

"We are trying to establish that right now, but at this stage the only connection we can see is that they've all lost somebody. I'm assuming that is how he targets his victims. There are no other similarities that we can see. Race, hair color, size—nothing. They've all been remarkably different."

"What about personality traits?" I ask, crossing my legs.

Ace nods. "We've looked into that, too. Again, no particular connection."

"So he's just what, scouring cemeteries looking for people who've lost loved ones? That just seems . . . too reckless for someone who is obviously thinking in great detail about what he's doing."

"Yeah, we're trying to figure out where he is finding these women."

I ponder that, and then something flickers into my mind. "What about funeral homes? Perhaps he is getting information from them?"

Ace nods. "It's possible. It isn't hard in this day and age to bribe someone out of information, it's a fairly easy task."

"Maybe he's going into the homes and bribing receptionists out of files, and just randomly picking?" I suggest.

"It is something I'll look into, but it seems he would be smarter than that, more precise. Any other ideas?"

I think about it.

"Maybe he simply reads death notices in the paper, or follows online groups where people go to support one another? I was on a few online groups, just talking to other people suffering the same as I was. They helped."

Ace nods again. "Those are both worth looking into, also. Could you get me the names of those online groups?"

"Sure," I say. "Another suggestion would be to look into support groups."

Ace studies me. "Ones that aren't online?"

"Yeah," I say. "I went to one a year or so after I lost Raymond—I just wasn't coping or moving forward. It really helped. There were a lot of men and women in those groups."

"Thank you, it's all worth looking into."

I feel a little better knowing I've contributed something. Even if they turn out to be dead ends.

I cross my arms, and rub my hands over them for a few seconds before asking, "Why do you think he's doing it? Targeting people who have lost someone?"

Ace keeps flicking through his notes, not looking up when he answers. "It usually goes back to childhood. Most serial killers follow a pattern, something that happened, something familiar to them. This man at some stage could have possibly lost someone, or maybe he experienced someone close to him changing due to the loss of someone. There will be a connection in there, somehow."

I nod, rubbing my arms still. "But you don't know what he actually does with these girls when he gets hold of them, before, he"—I swallow the hard lump in my throat—"kills them?"

Ace gives me a kind look, I'm sure he understands how terrifying it is for me to ask that question. "As far as we know, he doesn't harm them physically, but instead does damage mentally. When he's finished, he chokes them and then hangs them from a tree, with a bowtie around their necks."

A bowtie.

I shudder.

"Why a bowtie?"

Ace shakes his head again. "I'd say it would connect to whatever happened to him to make him this fucking crazy. It's a trademark—most killers have them."

"Does he, ah, rape them?"

"No," Ace says, his voice tight. "There has been no evidence of sexual assault. It's purely a mental torture. My guess is he holds them until he breaks them, and only when he's broken them does he kill them."

I press a hand to my thigh, rubbing frantically. It's not making me feel any better.

"It may not be the same thing," Ace tells me, his gaze dropping to the way my hand is frantically rubbing. "We're going to be talking to the victims' families tomorrow again, to see if we can get any solid answers."

"But right now you're assuming it is, right?"

"Better to be safe than sorry."

Right.

"We didn't know these other girls were being tormented because a lot of the time no one really knew about it. It wasn't until the third victim that we realized that all three had received messages like you have and had been put through the type of things you are going through. Serial killers are next to impossible to pinpoint. We got lucky here, Hartley. I know it doesn't seem like it, but we did. We got lucky because we may have figured it out before he took you."

"Do you think it'll deter him if he knows you have figured it out?"

Ace scratches a hand over the stubble on his jaw, before sighing and saying, "Honestly, I don't know. It'll either send him packing, or it'll make it more of a challenge. To have police officers searching everywhere for him, keeping his victim safe, it's possible that'll excite him. These people . . . they don't think like us."

Great, so I just became a hot commodity.

"Would you mind if I read about the other cases?" I dare to ask.

Ace studies me. "I'm not supposed to share that kind of thing, it's against the rules. But I'm going to bend them for you, because I know how I'd feel if I was in your situation. It's a terrifying thing."

"Thank you," I whisper.

He hands me three files. I hold them in my hands, and then, with a deep sigh, I read.

"I'm sorry, Jacob," I say to the man sitting on my sofa, hands in his lap. "It's just that right now I'm going through a really hard time, and I thought I might be ready for a relationship but after everything that's going on, I'm not. I really like you, and you've been so supportive, but I don't think I'm ready to take the next step."

Jacob's eyes hold mine, and I know I've upset him. I hate that I had to do that, but unfortunately my feelings for him aren't developing. I like him a lot. He's a great guy, one of the best, but he isn't the guy for me. I know that. Time isn't going to change that. I'm not the kind of girl to lead someone on in hopes I might develop something for him down the line. I'd never do that.

"I understand," Jacob says, his voice a little sad. "I wouldn't want you to enter into anything you're not ready for. I really like you, Hartley, but I won't force you to do this with me."

My heart hurts for him.

"I'm really sorry. I wish it could be different, but it just isn't right now."

Jacob stands with a nod. "We were mostly friends anyway, please don't concern yourself over it. I'm just happy to have met you."

"Can we stay friends, then?"

He smiles. "Of course we can. You can't get rid of me that easily."

I beam at him, and step forward for a hug when he comes in for one. "I'll call you soon, see how you're doing," he says, letting me go.

"That would be great, and I really am sorry."

He winks at me. "Don't be. Talk to you soon."

He leaves my apartment, and I lock the doors behind him. Only ten minutes later a knock sounds out. Narrowing my eyes, I rush over and call out, "Who is it?"

"Ah, it's Greg Jefferson."

Greg?

Should I open the door?

My gut twists. How did he find my apartment? How does he even know where to look? My skin prickles and I pull out my phone, preparing to dial Ace. "I'm sorry, I'm not opening the door," I say, double-checking the lock is fully in place.

"I'm not here to bother you . . ."

"How did you find my address?"

"I," he hesitates. "It isn't hard to find someone's address. I just want to talk, I promise I'm not here to make a scene."

It isn't hard to find someone's address?

What the hell?! Who just shows up to someone's apartment randomly?

"Please leave, I'm calling the police."

"That's what I wanted to talk about," he calls through the door. "They've called me in for an interview and I wondered why. They said it was in regards to you. What have you said about me?"

I'm uneasy. He might be telling the truth, he might have absolutely nothing to do with what's been going on, but the fact of the matter is that he's gone to the effort of finding out where I live, and coming over here. That doesn't sit right with me, and because of that, my uneasiness continues to grow.

"You need to leave. Police business is police business."

"I'd like to know what you're running around saying," he says, his voice a little harder than I'm comfortable with.

"I'm calling the police . . ." I say back.

"I don't know why you're creating trouble for me, but I won't have it . . ."

"Dialing right now!" I yell.

"I'm leaving," he snaps. "Be careful what stories you're spinning. I'd hate to get into trouble for something I didn't do."

I don't like this. At all.

I dial Ace once, but it goes to voicemail so I leave a quick message. "Ace, Greg came by my apartment and I didn't like how he was behaving. Can you call me?"

"Yeah, call the cops," Greg shouts. "Waste of my time, you were. If I get into trouble for something I haven't done, you'll pay."

I don't say anything more, I just wait, listening. I hear the door to the stairs slam, and only then do I unlock the door and peek outside. He's gone. My heart is racing. That wasn't normal. Not at all. The fact that he found my address makes me extremely uneasy.

I lock the door again, and wait for Ace to return my call. When he does, I inform him about Greg and he tells me he's moving the questioning forward—after he spent ten minutes demanding to know everything he said and dropping a few choice curse words at the audacity of Greg. Midway through our call, Taylor turns up, so I hang up with Ace, grateful my best friend is here right now. My heart is still racing from the encounter.

When Taylor skips in with two coffees and some muffins, it eases a little. I've been so busy with everything happening, I've hardly had the chance to talk to her. I haven't told her about Ace's suspicions yet, because he told me to keep it to myself as much as possible.

But she's my best friend.

I know I can trust her.

And I really need someone to talk to right now.

"Hey." I smile. "Gosh, I'm happy to see you."

"How is everything?" she asks, setting the coffees down.

"Greg just showed up."

She jerks and looks at me. "What? Why? How did he find your address?"

"I don't know, but he was going on about me getting him into trouble with the police. I told Ace, but I'm still really creeped out."

"Do you think he's behind this?"

I shrug. "I don't know, but it's all getting out of hand. It's been a crappy few days. I had to end it with Jacob today, too."

She spins around, giving me a look. "Why?"

I shrug. "Honestly, he was a really nice guy, but he just wasn't the guy for me. He was,—gosh, I'm going to sound like a terrible person for saying this—but he was just too nice. Don't get me wrong, I like nice, but . . . he just wasn't sparking anything inside me. At all."

She rolls her eyes. "You can't force chemistry."

"No, no you can't. Hey, listen, I need to talk with you about something else while I'm at it. I'm not really supposed to, but I need someone to talk this through with."

Her eyes widen, and she holds up a finger. "Okay, just let me get this out for us, then I'm sitting down, because I have a feeling I need to sit down by the look on your face."

I smile at her, and she nods. "Yep. Sit-down conversation."

She pulls two big double chocolate muffins from the bag and hands me one, then thrusts a coffee at me. I take both and we move to the chair and sit down, cross-legged, facing each other.

"Okay." She takes a sip of her coffee and a bite of her muffin. "Is this the kind of story that's going to make me cry, or scream, or do something violent?"

I give her a weak smile, because the idea of freaking her out bothers me, but I know if I don't tell her and she finds out from someone else, she'll flip out. She and I have always shared everything. Even the bad. Especially the bad. So, I take a deep breath, and just dive right in.

"Ace thinks he knows what's been happening with all these things going on, all Ray's stuff popping up . . ."

Her face goes slightly pale, because she knows me well enough by now to know that I'm not about to tell her everything is okay and we can stop worrying. No, she knows me well enough to know that I've sat her down for a reason.

"Hartley," she whispers. She hasn't used my full name in a long time. "What's going on?"

I take a deep breath and meet her eyes. "Ace thinks . . ." Just say it, Hartley. "Ace thinks it could be that serial killer who's been around recently."

The blood rushes from her face, and my heart aches. Is that how I looked when Ace told me? I place my muffin down, and my coffee, and reach over, taking her hand. "Breathe, Taylor."

"You're joking," she whispers. "This is a joke, right? It has to be. Tell me you're joking, please . . ."

I shake my head softly. "I'm not joking. We're going to figure it out, and I'll be fine."

She doesn't look convinced, and I don't blame her. I know exactly what she's thinking, what she's feeling, I went through the exact same emotions. Soon, even long after she's left my house, she'll go over every possible scenario in her head. She'll analyze, she'll pull it to pieces, she'll think of every single thing that could go wrong, and it'll lodge itself firmly in her heart, too. Where it won't leave.

Just like it did to me.

"Greg just came to your apartment, and the people who were supposed to be watching you didn't notice, and you're trying to tell me it's fine . . ."

She makes a point, and I make a note to mention to Ace that Greg seemed to get into the building without any problems. Ace said he was monitoring who was coming in and out, so someone must have missed something. That doesn't make me feel safe, in fact it makes me worry even more. I am relying on these people to keep danger away—if they don't do their job . . . danger can get in, and that thought terrifies me.

"It's okay, it'll be okay," I say, not sure I actually believe that.

"Hart," she whispers, reaching over and catching both my hands in hers. "I'm scared."

My bottom lip trembles, as I hold her eyes. "Me too, honey."

"If something happened to you . . ."

I squeeze her hands. "Ace isn't going to let that happen."

She nods, but her eyes are glassy.

I scoot closer, and she throws her arms around me, and together we sit like that for what seems like eternity, hanging onto each other. I'm scared. Scared out of my mind. I can be strong. I can keep it together. But the looming threat over my head, the possibility that I might not make it out of this unscathed, has every fear and insecurity I've ever had in my life rising to the surface.

It's getting into my head.

Which is exactly what he wants.

I can't let him win. I can't let him get into the deepest depths of my soul. I can't let him break me. I know what he wants. I know the satisfaction he's going to gain, and I have to make sure he doesn't ever gain that power. I have to make sure that I never, ever let him win. I need to find my strength, wrap both hands around it, and fight this.

"It's going to be okay," I tell Taylor. "I'm not going to let this person get to me."

"I won't let him get to you either," she sniffles, pulling back. "I'll become a serial killer and get him back, if I have to. I'm prepared to do whatever it takes. Only, my trademark will be, like, epic."

I laugh softly. Trust Taylor to be able to make light of even the darkest situation.

"I'm sure you'll do an amazing job." I smile at her. "Seriously, I wouldn't cross you."

She nods, and swipes a tear away. "That fucker will not get my best friend."

"No honey," I say, hugging her again, "he won't."

Right?

EIGHTEEN

"I want you to watch, as you might be able to help us out with any questions we haven't asked," Ace tells me, sitting me on the one side of a two-way mirror that looks into an interrogation room where the three men I went on dates with sit. "If you have something you need to say, just press this buzzer here."

Ace points to a little button on the control panels on this side of the room. I nod, taking a seat in a high-back leather chair.

"What are you going to ask them?" I say, meeting his eyes.

"Just some basic questions. I've done full background checks on them, and they all seem clean, but that doesn't mean they're not capable of pulling this off. Greg did come to your apartment, and that raises suspicion."

"Did you find out how he got in?"

"The police officer watching was on the phone and had his back turned. He got a verbal warning and was reassigned. I promise you protection is up to scratch now, Hartley."

I nod. "Okay."

He focuses back on the three men sitting in the room.

"You think Jacob is a suspect?" I ask, staring at Jacob through the glass and feeling bad he has to put up with this. Poor guy. He's probably regretting dating me right about now.

"I have to question anyone involved in your life, even briefly. Just to cover everything."

Fair enough. I make a note to apologize profusely to Jacob later. Even though I ended it, he's still been a good friend to me and was there for me when I needed him.

"I'll question Jacob first, he said he has a deadline. Then it'll be that balding fuck that has now pissed me off."

I stare at Greg. "Yeah."

Ace stares at the man, and then grunts. "What the fuck were you thinkin' goin' on a date with him? You're a gorgeous woman, Hartley."

My cheeks flush.

Did Ace just call me gorgeous?

"It was, ah, a blind date. So you don't get to see a picture, you just trust they're telling the truth about their looks. He lied about basically everything on his profile so he could get a young, attractive date. He didn't seem dangerous, but I guess anyone can be dangerous and not look it, right?"

Ace nods. "Yeah, sometimes it's the most normal-looking, kind ones that are the worst. I'll question him right after Jacob, purely because I don't like the fucker."

I bite my lip to stop from smiling as Ace glares at the man through the glass. Then he looks down at me, and his eyes drop to my lips. "Stop biting your lip, it isn't funny."

I release my lip and smile up at him.

"Christ," he murmurs. "Press the button if you need me."

Then he turns and walks out, slamming the door a little too hard. Moody. What did I do? Shrugging, and feeling pretty important right about now, I turn and face the glass that lets me see clearly into the other room where Ace has just entered. A police officer escorts Richard and Greg out. Ace sits across from Jacob and the two hold eyes. Oh boy.

I listen in as Ace attempts to exchange pleasantries with Jacob. Then he gets right into questioning him. "What made you want to go on a dating site?"

Jacob, whose hands are calmly placed in front of him, holds Ace's eyes without concern. "Why does anyone go on a dating site? We're looking for companionship, love, even just friendship. I haven't met anyone recently, so I thought I'd give it a go."

"You're a good-looking man, why haven't you been able to meet anybody?"

"Have you experienced the dating world lately, Detective? It is brutal. Women going for older, richer men, men going for young, attractive women—you try sitting in a club and attempting to meet a normal person. It isn't as easy as you might think. At least with online dating, you have the chance to narrow it down, just a little."

Ace studies him, eyes narrowed. "What made you pick Hartley's profile?"

Jacob smiles, warmly. "It sounded upbeat, and it

made her sound funny, and easygoing, all of which she is."

Aw.

"And had you been on any dates prior?"

"Two," Jacob says calmly. "Neither of them worked out."

"Interesting," Ace murmurs. "What about previous relationships?"

"We've all had previous relationships, Detective. I'm no different. I had a couple that lasted a few years, then fizzled out. It happens. I'm looking for long term, I don't wish to keep wasting a couple of years at a time."

"And you'd be happy to give me the names of those women?"

"Of course," Jacob says without hesitation.

"Have you had any previous criminal activity?"

Jacob shrugs. "You already know the answer to that, Detective. After all, you would have already checked me out."

I bite my lip and keep watching.

"Indeed," Ace murmurs again.

They go over a few other basic things, like Jacob's work, his friends. Jacob answers with ease and confidence. He also asks him where he was the nights of the break-ins, and Jacob was able to provide an alibi for them.

When he's done, he releases Jacob and calls in Greg—who looks absolutely terrified. A light sheen of sweat covers his forehead.

"Gregory Jefferson, I'm Detective Henderson and I'd like to ask you a few questions today about Hartley Watson."

I have to admit, Ace in detective mode is kind of hot.

Greg nods, rubbing his hands together nervously.

"Everything you say will be recorded."

Greg nods again, and then stammers, "Look, I didn't mean to go to her apartment. I freaked out when I heard your voicemail. I'd never hurt her, I swear."

"How did you find her address, Greg?"

"It isn't hard to find someone's address, Detective. I had no ill intentions."

"You practically threatened her."

"I was angry, that's all. I was nervous, too."

"What for?"

Greg shifts. "I know I upset her, I thought maybe she was trying to put some false charges on me, or something like that, because she was disgusted with me. I . . . I got accused of doing something I didn't do when I was younger, and because of that I'm a little sensitive. I know exactly how easily a woman could make out that I've done something I haven't."

Ace narrows his eyes. "What did you get accused of?"

Greg shifts. "It never went further than a verbal accusation, that was dropped, so I don't think it matters."

Ace makes a sound deep in his throat. "Very well. Tell me why you think Hartley would be disgusted with you, as you say? What would make her feel like that?"

"She, ah, got upset at me."

Ace looks up, pinning the man with his stare. Even I squirm in my seat. "Why did she get upset with you? I'm asking for you to answer. Now answer."

"I may have lied about being young, and, ah, handsome."

Ace cocks a brow. "Why would you do that, Greg?"

"I just didn't think anyone would give me a chance if I didn't," Greg splutters. "Not all of us are blessed with good looks, like yourself."

"So you lied to get a girl to go on a date with you. You deceived her."

"I didn't do it in a bad way, I swear," Greg cries out, placing his hands on his lap.

"Why not just tell her the truth?" Ace continues, unfazed by Greg's clear outburst of panic. "Why tell her a lie? Is there a particular reason, or is just that you didn't think she'd go out with you?"

"I didn't know it would be Hartley I met. It could've been be anyone. That's why it's called a blind date."

Ace nods, writing something. "And what happened when Hartley found out you had lied to her?"

"She was upset. She told me I was shallow, said a few colorful words, and left."

"You weren't angry at her?"

Greg looks sheepish. "My ego was bruised, so yes, I was a little mad. Like I said, I thought maybe she had lied about me doing something inappropriate, when I didn't . . ."

"Lying to get young girls is inappropriate."

"I'm not a terrible man. I'm not."

Ace studies him. "Did she talk to you about her husband, by any chance?"

Greg swallows, and I can see he is trying to figure out how to answer the question. He obviously doesn't want to lie, but he doesn't want to put his foot right in the middle of it either. "Yes, she told me she'd lost her husband."

He goes with the truth. Good for him.

"What did you think when she told you that?"

"I felt sad for her."

"Nothing else?"

Greg shakes his head.

"Okay, Greg. Thank you for your time, I'll call you if I require any further answers."

An officer comes in and escorts Greg out of the room. Ace walks out, too, and is back with me a couple of minutes later. "He's still on the suspect list, but I'm not sure it's him."

I raise my brows. "You can tell that already?"

Ace nods. "Unless he's the world's best actor, then yes, I can tell that already. The guy looked like he might pass out. Doesn't mean he isn't capable of doing it, but I'm not convinced. I think he probably came to your apartment purely because he was afraid you were going to try and get him in trouble. I'm keeping an eye on him, though."

Damn.

"And Jacob?"

Ace grunts. "Don't like the man, but he's clean, too."

"Wow." I nod, thoughtfully. "You're good."

"Best at my job," he says, his voice strong and determined. "Bringing the other one in now. You enjoying yourself?"

I look up to see an almost playful expression. I have to blink a few times, but no, I'm definitely seeing it right. My heart swells, and I shoot him a big smile.

"I actually feel pretty important. I have never been able to do something like this, or even watch something like this. It's fascinating."

He raises half his mouth in . . . is that a smile? Then he turns and disappears out of the room before I can think about it anymore. With a racing heart, I glance back at the room and watch as they bring poor Richard in. He looks even more nervous than Greg. I bet these guys are kicking themselves for having met me. Poor things.

Ace goes over the same introduction with Richard, and then flies right into the questions about Raymond, and if I spoke about him. Richard keeps calm, telling Ace exactly what went down on the date, even right down to the fact that I spent three hours comforting him over the breakup with his ex-girlfriend, whom he was now seeing again. Go Richard.

Ace dismisses him, writes a few more notes, before joining me again.

I swivel around on the chair when he comes in. "So?"

Ace shakes his head. "I'd also be very surprised if it's him. We'll keep them on the list, but I don't think any of them is our guy. I'm starting to think you were just a random choice, maybe in the wrong place at the wrong time—which could very likely be a support group, however it is still a random choice. You had to have stood out to him for whatever reason. It's possible you've never physically encountered this man in your life."

My heart sinks.

"What about the other victims. Did you talk to their families?"

He nods. "As far as I can tell, all three of the girls

didn't have any family close by. Two of them didn't have parents. That's the only real connection outside of the fact that they've all lost someone, that I can make."

"He's targeting people who don't have anyone to talk to about it."

Those poor people, suffering on their own.

"Yeah, they had friends, but mostly they were on their own. It's why he managed to get away with tormenting them for so long. By the time anyone figured out what was happening, it was too late."

I shiver. "What about me? I mean, I know I don't have family around, but I have Taylor, and, I mean, I live right next door to you."

"He could be bored," Ace says, crossing his arms. "He might be stepping up the game, giving himself a bit more of a challenge."

Great.

Just great.

"So where does that leave us now?"

Ace exhales slightly. "We keep looking, keep talking to people, keep trying to figure out anything that can point us in the right direction. We've got an eye on every aspect of your life. We'll find him."

"And if you don't?"

"We will."

He's so sure of himself.

I know I should believe in him, and I really, really want to.

But until that man is locked behind bars, I don't think I'll believe in anything.

"How are you doing?" Jacob asks over the phone as I walk from my apartment over to Ace's.

Ace invited me over for dinner, so we could go through some more information on the case to see if we could come up with something together. I didn't say no because I'm enjoying spending time with him and, honestly, I feel safer there. I feel good knowing he's right there if anything should happen.

"I'm doing okay," I tell Jacob, reaching out and knocking on Ace's door. "Things are still the same, but I'm safe. How have you been?"

"Great," he tells me. "I've been busy at work. I'm sorry I haven't called. I wanted to give you some space, I know you've been stressed."

The door swings open and Ace appears, wearing a casual gray tee and a pair of exercise shorts. I swallow, and try to avert my eyes, because damn, he looks hot.

"No problem," I tell Jacob, far too distracted by the hot man standing right in front of me, making everything inside me spark to life. What the hell is this? "Listen, I'd love to chat, but I'm meeting with Ace. We are going over some notes. Can I give you a call tomorrow?"

"Of course," Jacob says. "I'm glad to hear you're doing well. We'll catch up soon."

"We will. 'Night, Jacob."

" 'Night, Hart."

I hang up the phone, and my eyes move up Ace's body until they meet his.

"You still talking to that dick?"

I bite my lip to force back a laugh. Ace doesn't miss it, and those gorgeous eyes roll up to the ceiling. "It's not fuckin' funny. You could just answer me instead of laughing."

"You're so moody," I giggle softly, stepping past

him and walking into his apartment. "Honestly, Ace, who cares who I talk to?"

He doesn't answer, he just locks the door. "Whatever makes you happy."

I laugh again and walk over, taking a seat at his kitchen counter, staring over at him when he walks in and asks, "Have you eaten?"

"No, not yet. I thought maybe we could order something."

He cocks a brow. "That so?"

"Yeah, big guy," I say, crossing my arms. "That's so."

He seems amused by my comment. He doesn't react to it, but I can see it in his eyes, the way they dance. It's nice to see him lighten up a little. He's always so serious.

"What do you want?" he asks, pulling out a heap of menus he has in a little menu holder by the wall. "Pizza, pasta, Chinese, Indian . . ."

Jesus.

"I'm a fan of Indian food," I say, gauging his reaction. "Or Chinese. Or food, in general."

He nods and flicks the Chinese and Indian menus towards me. "Here, pick one. I'm going to have a shower, I just got back from the gym."

The thought of Ace in the shower, all that water, and that body . . . has my cheeks going pink. He doesn't say anything, but I don't miss his eyes scanning briefly over my warm cheeks before he turns and disappears down the hall. "Order something," he calls out.

Right.

Bossy.

I go with Indian and order a few different dishes

and some rice. The woman on the other line snaps at me that it'll be half an hour, and then hangs up without even a good bye. Well, unless the food is fantastic I won't be ordering from there again. I stand once I'm done, and move into Ace's living room, checking everything out. There are no pictures that I can see, which just sparks my curiosity even more.

I walk back into the kitchen and towards the sink, when I notice a picture on his laptop. A gorgeous blonde fills the screen, her beautiful smiling face lighting it up in a way I've never seen before. She has something about her, something fresh and beautiful. Her eyes are bright, and as blue as the sky, but mostly they're warm. She looks like a loving lady, the best kind. My heart aches for Ace.

Obviously that's his wife.

I can see why he loved her, she's absolutely beautiful.

I get myself some water, and send a text to Taylor while I wait for Ace to finish. A knock at the door about ten minutes later has my head whipping up. Jesus, that was the fastest Indian food I've ever ordered. I glance down the hall. The shower has only just stopped, so I'm guessing Ace will be another few minutes. Shrugging, I walk over and unlock it, opening it to find . . . nobody.

I poke my head out and glance left and right. There is no one there. I'm about to close the door when I look down and see some bags of food placed by the door. How rude. They could have at least waited until we opened the door. What if it was the wrong apartment? I reach for the food but stop, hand outstretched, when I realize it's not Indian food.

My heart launches into my mouth, and for a moment I'm frozen there, half bent down to get the food. It takes me a few seconds to gather myself enough to pick up the bag with shaky hands and step back inside the apartment. I lock the door and walk numbly to the kitchen. "Food here already?" Ace asks, but I can't answer him.

I just stare at the bag.

I already know what will be inside. Two orders of cashew chicken. One of fried rice. It was Raymond's and my favorite meal. We used to get it every Friday night, without fail, and we'd sit and eat it while watching reruns of *Grey's Anatomy*. My hands shake, and the bag kind of *plonks* down onto the kitchen counter.

"Hartley?"

"I didn't order this, Ace," I whisper. "But I know who did . . ."

Ace moves quickly, walking over and snatching the bag from the counter, jerking it open and staring inside. He comes up with a note, and quickly unfolds it. He reads it out loud, but most of it falls on deaf ears. I can already see it's in Ray's handwriting, and I already know what it'll say. Raymond used to send me food all the time if he was working late, and knew he couldn't be here.

> *I'm sure you've had a stressful week and will enjoy your favorite.*
>
> Love, R x

"I'm making a call," Ace says. "Sit tight."

I wasn't about to go anywhere. I stand for a few minutes, gathering myself, and then I turn towards

Ace, who has the phone to his ear. I realize when he starts speaking that he's talking to the Chinese place the food arrived from.

"Yes, I'm a detective. You had someone in the last half an hour order two orders of cashew chicken and a fried rice."

He listens.

"Yes, correct. Can you tell me anything about that person?"

He listens some more.

"Was it a male or a female? Did that person come and pick it up?"

He curses.

"Right, and you're sure?"

A mumble and then an exhale. He hangs up the phone and turns to me. "She told me a homeless-looking man came in and ordered the food, then came back to pick it up. She doesn't know who he was. This man isn't stupid—he made sure this couldn't be traced back to him. He must've paid the homeless guy money to do his dirty work."

God.

This just keeps getting worse. "How did he know I was here, Ace?"

Ace rubs a hand over his face, clearly as frustrated and confused as I am with the whole situation. "I'm not sure. He could have been watching the building, he could have seen through my windows. It isn't hard, we face the main road. There could be many reasons. For all we know, he walked down the hall and heard our voices."

I shiver, thinking that he might have been that close. "What do we do now?"

Ace shakes his head. "Nothing we can do. There

is absolutely no lead. He made sure of it. Don't stress, we'll throw this food out and wait for our real order. You're safe here."

"I'm starting to think I'm not safe anywhere."

He gives me a look that says he understands. "Sit down. We'll eat when the order arrives, and try to figure out where to go from here."

"Ace," I say, walking over and sitting on his couch. "Do you think you could set him up?"

Ace looks to me, contemplating that. "It's something we could probably look into."

"I mean, if he's playing games, I wonder if we could set him up and trap him somehow . . ."

"Wouldn't be easy. He's smart, he's probably onto every trick in the book, but it is something I'll think about."

"It was just an idea," I say, crossing my legs. "I don't know much about any of this, all I know is that I want it to go the hell away. I don't sleep anymore."

"I have sleeping pills, if you want one."

I study him as he shuts his laptop down, then joins me on the sofa. It's only then I really pay attention to his attire. Or lack of. He's wearing those long pajama bottoms again, and nothing else. His bronze chest is bare, and shining from his recent shower. He looks . . . God, he looks amazing. I swing my eyes away and stare at the television that he's just turned on. Suddenly more than aware that we're alone together. I wonder if he can feel the tension I feel?

"I don't think I'll take any pills," I finally manage. "Thank you, though."

He glances at me from the corner of his eyes. "Breathe."

"What?" I say. "I am."

"You're holding your breath."

He's right, I am. I exhale in a rush. "How do you pick up on so much?"

"I'm a detective. It's my job to not only watch how people react and behave, but also to work fully off my instinct. I'm good at it. I pick up on tiny little things people do when they're nervous, or anxious, or scared, whatever it might be."

"So you're like a body language expert?"

He snorts. "Wouldn't go that far. I just know when people are feeling certain things by the way they act."

"Really?" I challenge. "What am I feeling right now then?"

"You're nervous because I'm sitting here without a shirt. You've looked at my body three times now. I'd bet any money your heart is racing. You're also terrified by what just happened. You've rubbed your hands over your shorts twice, before fumbling them together in your lap."

I blink, and then glance down to where my hands are indeed fumbling together in my lap.

"I didn't look at you three times!"

I did. I really did.

"Yes you did," he says, eyes still on the television. "You just looked again."

I clamp my eyes shut. "You're starting to freak me out now."

He makes a sound that almost could be passed off as a chuckle. "I'm not the one staring at you. I'm starting to think you have a problem when it comes to staring."

"I don't," I point out. "I just . . . I pay attention."

He grunts.

Whatever.

"Just put something on the television and stop talking."

He glances at me again, this time with a brow raised. "You're a bossy thing, aren't you?"

"Coming from the king of bossy, I take that as a compliment."

Another grunt.

"At least you know how to use your manners these days."

Those eyes roll upwards.

"And stop rolling your eyes, it's rude."

He looks over to me, dead on this time. "If you weren't such a fuckin' pain in the ass, I wouldn't have to be rude."

I grin at him. "I was always polite to you, Ace."

"You waved at me like a crazy person once, out of the blue, just right there in my face. I thought you were nuts. What would you have me do?"

My mouth drops open. "When someone waves to you, you wave back, even if they are nuts. And it wasn't right in your face . . ."

One brow cocks.

Okay, I did pretty much wave right up in his space. "I only did it because you refused to pay any attention to me. I tried over and over to say hello, or to be nice, but you just ignored me."

"Stop taking it so personally."

I huff.

"I'll get you up to scratch on your neighbor skills one of these days."

"You're here, on my couch, bitching in my ear, aren't you?"

I smirk. "Indeed I am."

"Then I'd say I'm doing fairly well. Now be quiet so I can watch television."

I keep the smirk, but I go quiet and turn, watching the television and feeling okay for the first time in weeks. Not better, definitely not safe, but okay. And right now, "okay" is everything.

"Okay" is just what I need to get me through.

NINETEEN

"Order up," my boss, Jayme, calls, sliding a plate across the counter at me.

I rush over and take it, trying to ignore the car sitting across the street with a police officer inside, staring right in here, watching me.

"What's the cop for?" coworker, Dani, asks as she takes the next order that's served up.

"I'm not really sure," I lie.

"He's been sitting there all night."

"Yeah."

She stares at me for a moment, her long red hair tied high on her head. I like working with Dani, she's friendly. I'm not overly close with her, but when I was going through a fitness craze, we used to go on a morning run together. She's fit, and funny, and easy to work with.

"Strange," she murmurs. "I'm about to finish up my shift and then you have crazy on."

I sigh.

The other girl who works with us, Rebecca, is a

total cow. She's older, and thinks she's entitled to the world because of that. She's had a problem with me since I started here, and the few times I've been unfortunate enough to be scheduled with her, she makes my life hell. I'm not sure what it is she doesn't like about me, but she makes her feelings clear.

"Speak of the devil," Dani murmurs, leaning in close as the older blonde appears from the back room, tying an apron around her waist. "That's my cue."

"I hate you," I mouth to Dani, and she flashes me a smile before clocking out for the night.

I keep serving tables, trying to stay out of Rebecca's way when she breezes past me, shouldering me when I get too close.

"Order up," Jayme yells again, and I rush over.

Rebecca appears before I can reach the plates and slides them off the counter.

"Those plates are for my section," I say, staring at her.

"Well, those people are hungry and waiting. By the time it takes you to pick up your feet and get the plates, they're already writing a terrible review online about customer service."

"Seriously? I was walking straight over here," I say, trying to keep calm. I need this job. What I don't need is her attitude.

"Yes 'seriously'," she snaps. "If you're not going to put your best foot forward, maybe you should look for other jobs."

"Last time I checked, Rebecca, you aren't my boss."

I take the plates from her hand and she glares at me.

"What is your problem?" I say, feeling the stress of the last few weeks bubble up.

"My problem is you. I'm constantly having to run around after you, and pick up after you, and do everything because you're not paying attention. And everyone feels sorry for you, because oh no, you lost your husband. That was years ago. Some of us have a job to do, bills to pay, and don't need to play the pity game to get ahead."

I blink at her.

She did not just say that . . . did she?

"I'm not using my situation to do anything. I work just as hard as you."

"No. You. Don't. You're the favored one. You think you work hard, but really, you get everything easy. Just handed to you."

Talk about resentment. I'm not in the mood for this, and I'm certainly not in the mood to lose my job, so I turn on my heel and walk off.

Then I avoid her for the rest of the night.

Honestly. I can't take much more.

When my shift is over, I pack my things, ignoring Rebecca's glares in my general direction, and head out and over to the police car. Jayme asked me what was going on, and I simply told her he was a friend, though I know she didn't believe me. I was hardly going to tell her I might have a serial killer looking for me and she should be concerned. I'd lose my job. And right now I need it—with my school and bills, I couldn't be without work.

I greet the officer as I climb in, and stay silent the entire ride home, wondering what the hell crawled up Rebecca's ass and died. I know she doesn't like me, but honestly, to be angry because she thinks I'm getting special treatment because I lost my husband is unfair. I'm not getting special treatment, I work just as hard as anyone in that place. Jayme runs a tight ship, and yes she likes me, but she'd never let me slack off.

I wonder what Rebecca's problem is.

When we arrive at my apartment, the officer says, "I'll just check the house."

I nod and unlock the door, letting him in. He strides into the living room, eyes scanning. I step in behind him, but stop and look down. There is a slip of paper underneath my door. That cold feeling washes over my body as I lean down and pick it up. I flip it open and my body goes completely numb. The handwriting, I could swear, was my husband's. The perfect strokes, the way the letters curl instead of end sharply.

My hands shake as I read the words.

I don't like you being alone tonight. Make sure you lock those doors.

Love, R x

I wince and scrunch the letter in my hand, trying to fight back my tears. The officer on duty comes out, not looking at me as he says, "It's all clear, there is no one here. I'll be waiting outside the door until Ace finishes his shift. Will that be all?"

I should tell him about the note I have crushed in my hand, but if I open my mouth right now I'm going to lose it. I just know it. So I give him a nod, and somehow force my lips to spread into a weak, pathetic smile. He doesn't seem to notice anything is wrong, and gives me a nod before stepping outside the door. I lock it behind him, and then the tears come. They roll down my cheeks and I sink to my knees, silently sobbing.

Why me?

Why won't this man leave me the hell alone?

Why is he torturing me?

I crawl down the hall, the letter still stuffed in my hand. I drop it at some point, and through my hysterical crying manage to reach my shower and strip off, crawling in and turning it on as hot as I can stand it. Then I bring my knees up to my chest, and I lose it. I absolutely lose it. I'm terrified. The ache in my chest just won't leave. It doesn't matter what I do, I can't get rid of it. It hangs around, tormenting me, constantly reminding me that I'm in serious danger.

It's the thought that this killer might just get hold of me that has the hysterical crying turning into pants. Short, harsh pants. It doesn't matter how many police officers are by my side, there is still a small window of opportunity for this man to slip in. And if he does, if he gets hold of me, he could end my life. The very thought of my life hanging so heavily under threat, terrifies me.

People are right when they say you think of everything you should be doing when something happens that could threaten your very existence. I've been holding back for the last four years, mourning for Raymond, but I should have been living. Hell, he'd want me to live. He would want me to be out there, enjoying life, traveling—hell, even falling in love. But I've kept it all at arm's length, terrified to live again, terrified to hurt again.

Now I may not get any of that.

My head drops into my arms and I cry so hard my body shakes. I'm making so many ugly sounds, I don't hear the shower door open, I don't realize anyone is in my bathroom until two solid arms come around me, and I'm being scooped up. A startled scream escapes my throat, followed by more hysterical sobs. "Hush," he murmurs. "It's me."

Ace?

He carries me out of the shower, jerking a towel off the railing as he goes. He wraps it around me, as best he can, and then sits us down on the bed, me nestled in his lap, his big thighs encasing my bottom, his arms wrapped around my body, securing me in, and his chest pressing against me, making me feel safe. I turn and nuzzle into him, pressing my cheek against his pec and sobbing. I can't stop it. I don't even think I should.

I'm so afraid.

Ace doesn't say anything, he just holds onto me as I break in his arms. Occasionally his fingers run down my hair, or stroke over my shoulder. I tremble and sob, clutching onto him for dear life, not wanting him to let go, because right now, he's the only person who makes me feel safe. After a good twenty minutes of crying, my tears slowly start to subside, and I start the hiccupping every few seconds, as my body tries to calm itself.

"It's going to be okay, Hartley," he murmurs into my hair. "I won't let anyone hurt you."

I hiccup again.

"I know you're afraid, I know you're carrying around something nobody can understand, but I need you to trust me."

A nod. Then another hiccup.

"You have to be strong. You have to keep it together. This is what he wants. This is him trying to break you. Do not let him break you. You've been through what is, without a doubt, the hardest thing any person can endure in life—losing someone you love. You got through that, and you carried on with your life. Don't let him win now."

Don't let him win now.

Don't let him win.

I nod and mindlessly press my lips to Ace's chest. The cotton of his shirt meets them, making me realize what I just did. I jerk back and look up at him. He's studying me, and the look on his face is one I can't read. It's soft, yet it holds the same broodiness it always has, but it's what's behind his eyes that captures me. Affection. I can see it, so very clearly. A deep affection. A deep affection aimed at me.

"I won't let him win," I croak.

He nods, but those eyes stay locked on mine. "Good girl."

He lifts me off his lap, and I want to whine and cling to him, but I don't. I let him carefully move me and place me down onto the soft mattress we're sitting on. I tuck the towel around me, and only now realize he just saw me naked. My cheeks burn at the thought, and I stand on shaky legs and move to my closet, grabbing a pair of cotton shorts and a tank.

I duck into the bathroom, get changed, brush my hair and teeth, and then slip back out. Ace is still sitting on my bed, and he's studying the note I dropped in the hall when I had my little meltdown. I join him back on the bed, staring at the letter in his hands. "That handwriting is identical to Raymond's."

Ace nods. "It isn't hard for people to learn how to copy someone's handwriting, it's how people forge signatures. Now come on, you need to take your mind off it."

"I'm sorry, about all of this. I've had a really bad night. There is a girl at work and she just made my night miserable."

"Did you put her name on the list of people for me to check out?"

I nod. "Yes. She did say something about me being entitled because I lost my husband. Do you think she might have something to do with this?"

Ace shrugs. "It could be anyone, or it could be a perfect stranger. Either way, I'll look into her."

I nod, tucking my legs up to my chest. A long, drawn-out yawn escapes my throat. I'm so tired. I'm starting to wonder when the last time I had a decent sleep was.

"You need to get some sleep," Ace says, studying me, tucking the note into his pocket.

"I can't," I whisper. "I try and try, but I just can't sleep. Even if you're in my house, even if Taylor is . . . I just can't sleep."

He nods and then stands, pulling his shirt from the top of his pants. I watch, my mouth slightly agape, as he pulls it over his head and tosses it on the floor. Then he makes light work of his pants, stripping down until he's wearing only his boxer briefs. "Which is your side?"

I blink.

He stares at me expectantly. "Which is your side, Hartley?"

"What are you doing?" I whisper.

"I'm getting into this bed, so I can get some sleep.

I could sleep for a year with the shifts I've been working, and you're afraid, so it's a win-win. Now which side is yours?"

"You're going to . . . sleep . . . with me?"

He gives me that impatient look. "I'm not going to touch you, or try anything, I'm just going to be in here, because I know you'll sleep if I am."

I swallow.

Ace. In my bed.

In my bed.

Oh God.

"Isn't that against the rules or something?"

He raises his brows. "Since when do you care about the rules, and I'm off duty. Right now, we're just friends."

"We're friends?"

He makes an impatient sound and looks to the ceiling. Only after a few seconds of deep breathing, does he glance back down at me. "Are you going to ask questions all night, or are you going to let me get some sleep?"

"Right," I whisper. "I sleep on the left."

He nods, moving around to the right side of the bed, tossing the covers back, and sliding in. I stand at the end of the bed, lamely, just glancing down at him. He tucks his hands up behind his head, and then looks at me. "Are you going to stand there all night, or are you going to get in?"

I swallow.

Then I get in, laying my body right on the edge, nervous but not uncomfortable. I haven't slept in the same bed as a man for over four years. I don't know what it feels like anymore. What if I snore? Or worse? What if I grope him? What if I try to cuddle him? God. The possibilities of what I may do when sleeping are endless.

Before I can think too much more about it, an arm stretches across the bed, curling around my wrist, and then before I know what's happening, I'm being jerked closer to Ace. I gasp, and scramble backwards a little when he lets me go. "I don't bite," he murmurs. "Seriously, anyone would think you've never had a man in your bed."

"It's been a while," I tell him.

He glances at me. "For me, too."

Oh.

Suddenly, I feel better. So much better. Because he gets it. He understands. He might not be showing it in the way I am, but he knows exactly what I'm talking about. My body relaxes, and I study him as he pulls out his phone and sends a couple of text messages. "You're doing the staring thing again."

"That's because you're nice to stare at," I admit.

He glances away from the phone and looks at me. He doesn't say anything, he just takes me in for a minute, and then looks back to his phone. Already my eyes are getting heavy. I try to keep my focus on him, but having someone in my bed, knowing I'm safe, knowing that nobody can get in this room without Ace knowing, has my body relaxing for the first time in weeks.

Before I know it, I'm asleep.

But I could swear I hear him say in a low, whispered tone, "You're nice to stare at too, sweetheart."

But I think I'm dreaming.

I wake in the morning and there is something big, hard, and warm running up the entire length of my body from behind. For a moment, I panic, and then I remember that Ace was in my bed last night, and chose to sleep with me. I shift a little, but he's wrapped himself around me. One arm is slung over my waist, one of his legs is tangled through mine, and I can feel his breath tickling the back of my neck.

He's spooning me!

My heart races and for a long, long moment I don't know what to do. Should I move? Should I just stay here and enjoy how incredible it feels to have a man so close to me, wrapping me in his warmth? I shift, and I don't miss the hard length pressing against my bottom. Oh. My. God. Morning wood. My cheeks burn and I try to suppress the random giggle that climbs up my throat, but I can't hold it back.

It's so out of the blue, so completely strange, but it bursts from my mouth loud and cackling.

Ace shifts behind me, and that length rubs against my bottom, only increasing my giggles until I'm laughing.

"Are you laughing?" he murmurs in that sleepy, sexy voice all men have when they wake in the morning.

"You . . ." I inhale, trying to keep it together. "You have . . ."

"Morning wood."

I burst out into more hysterical laughter.

He obviously doesn't think it's funny.

"What is so funny about that?" he grumbles.

"You just . . . you just . . . I just . . ."

I can't breathe.

This is so embarrassing it's funny.

"All men get it, Hartley," he grunts. "No big deal."

No *big* deal.

Oh God.

I lose it. I'm crazy. It's official.

"No *big* deal, huh?" I say between pants of laughter.

"Jesus Christ," he grumbles. "You've lost it."

"I'm sorry. I don't even know why. I just, I don't know, it's funny."

"Still can't see how."

No. Neither can I. But do you think that'll stop the laughter?

He places a hand on my hip and thrusts forward. My laughter is strangled in my throat as a burst of pleasure shoots right to my core. My mouth drops open and holy crap, I think I might need a new set of panties.

"Now who's laughing?" he growls into my ear, before rolling away, leaving me aching in a place that hasn't ached for so many years.

Well.

Okay then.

I roll and watch as he climbs out of the bed, shoves one big hand into his boxers and adjusts himself, and then leans down and picks up his clothes. I lick my lips, and swallow a few times because my throat is dry. God, he's gorgeous. My body tingles as it recalls the very recent feeling he gave it, when he thrust that long, thick length against me. I shudder.

Get it together.

I force my body to move and slide out of the bed, throwing my legs over the side. I stand, not glancing at Ace again as I grab a robe and pull it around myself, before disappearing out of the room and into the kitchen. I turn the coffee maker on just as Ace comes out, fully dressed, running his fingers through his hair.

"Want a coffee?" I ask him.

"What are your plans for today? Do you have to work?" he responds, ignoring my actual question.

"Yeah, I work from lunchtime until after eight tonight."

"Good, I'll have someone outside to make sure you get in okay."

Okay then.

"So, coffee?"

He shakes his head. "I have to get going. I'll call in someone to wait at the door until you're ready for work. You going to be okay on your own?"

He's being weird.

I hate that.

Did my laughing make him feel uncomfortable? Or is he regretting staying the night? Maybe it made him feel strange. After all, he lost his wife not all that long ago. Maybe it's bringing back some painful memories. Deciding not to make a big deal of it because, after all, he's just taking care of me because it's his job, I smile and nod. "Okay, no problem."

He doesn't look at me as he pulls out his phone and makes a call, barking an order at the poor sod on the other side, telling whomever it is to come up and take watch at my door. Then he hangs up the phone, grabs his things, and leans a hip against the counter to wait.

"Call me when you're finished work," he murmurs, looking anywhere but at me. "So I know you're safe, I'll check in with the officers I have on duty."

Right.

"Okay," I say softly.

A knock sounds at the door a couple of minutes later, and without a good bye, Ace goes over to it, says something to the man on the other side, and then yells out "Lock the door" before leaving.

Well.

That was awkward.

And kind of painful.

What did I do wrong?

TWENTY

I stretch and yawn, glad my shift is over. It's past nine, and I worked a little longer than I anticipated. It was busier than usual, so when my boss asked if I could stay back a few hours, I happily agreed. It's more cash for me, and the tips were super tonight, so I earned a little more than I usually would for the week. I walk out front of the restaurant and stand under the streetlight, pulling out my phone. I'm right near the door, so I figure I'm safe enough here.

The police officer watching me left about five minutes ago, as Ace is on his way. He told me to stay inside the restaurant until Ace arrived. I agreed, even though here I am standing out front, but I can hear my boss's voice behind me. She's standing at the door chatting to a lingering customer. I highly doubt anyone will jump out and grab me right now. I shoot Taylor a message while I wait for Ace.

H: Hey chicky. I miss you. How are you?

She responds right away.

T: Good, busy. I have all these assessments going right now. Boo! I wanted to come over tonight, but I have taken tomorrow night off so I can come and stay with you. How are you?

H: I'm doing okay. Getting there.

T: I'm glad. Listen, I'm in class atm. I'll call you tonight?

H: Perfect! Xo

I tuck my phone away and wait. Five minutes turns into ten, and Ace still isn't here. I glance down at the time—yep, he should be here by now. The station isn't that far away from where I work, and he told the other officer he was nearly here. I pull out my phone again and call him. It goes to voicemail. I try again. Nothing.

Sighing, I tuck it back away and wait another fifteen minutes. Something has obviously held him up, and I really want to get home. I glance over to the street where my car is parked. It's just across the road. I'll lock the doors when I get in and wait for him at home, but I really need to pee, and shower, and I'm tired. I contemplate it for a minute, glancing around. There doesn't seem to be anyone nearby. I try calling Ace once more, and when he doesn't answer, I turn and call out to my boss, "I'm going to leave. If someone comes asking for me, tell him I've gone home! I'll see you tomorrow."

She waves. "No problem, hon. Good night."

"Night!"

I walk out the front doors and glance over at the parking lot that holds my car. I've been parking closer since the last incident. My phone beeps with a text just as I'm about to reach for my keys. I pull it out and glance at it, walking and reading the text from Taylor. I respond as I walk.

By the time I get to the car, I haven't yet pulled out my keys. I usually have them in my hand before I even walk out the doors. I immediately dig around for them. A noise distracts me, causing me to jerk my head up. I glance around, but I can't see anyone. Something uneasy washes over me, and my movements become frantic, as I dig around in my purse for my keys.

Why is there so much shit in here?

Another noise has my head whipping around. It sounds like someone is close by. I quickly scan the other cars, but can't see anything or anyone around. My heart kicks into overdrive. This was a bad idea. Dammit, where the hell are my keys? I shove my hand so hard into my purse it drops to the ground, scattering items everywhere.

"Dammit!" I hiss, dropping down to my knees and picking up as much as I can.

The sound of boots crunching has my heart launching into my throat. This was definitely a bad idea. What was I thinking? Anyone could take me. Dammit. Panic seizes me as my fingers fumble around with the items on the ground, picking them up as quickly as I can. When I hear another noise, closer this time, I decide screw it. I find my keys, and pick them up along with my phone and house keys. All the other little things can stay there.

I stand quickly, eyes scanning around once more.

I can't see anyone, but I can feel it. Someone is watching me. Panic grips my chest again, tightening it until I feel like I can't breathe. I shove the key into the car door and unlock it, practically throwing my body into the driver's seat. I shut the door quickly and lock it, and for a moment I sit there, panting, eyes darting around the parking lot.

Someone is out there.

I know they are.

I start the car and back out quickly, not wanting to look around a second longer. Only when I pull out onto the main road, do I exhale. Oh God. Was he there? Was he right there? Would he have taken me? What in the hell was I thinking? I shouldn't have gotten distracted by my phone and had my keys in my hands, like I always do. It was absolutely incredibly stupid of me to do something so unsafe when my life is on the line. And where the hell is Ace?

I'm an idiot.

An absolute idiot.

My hands tremble the entire way home, and when I pull up at the apartment complex, I just sit in my car, doors locked, too afraid to get out. I'm not risking walking up there on my own. I shouldn't have even gotten into this car on my own. I dig through my purse, grateful I didn't lose the pepper spray when I dropped it. I curl my fingers around the pepper spray and bring it close to my chest. Then I put my phone in my other hand. And I just wait.

The phone ringing ten minutes later has a scream launching out of my throat. With shaky fingers, I glance at the display. It's Ace. I answer it without hesitation. "Ace?"

"Where. The. Fuck. Are. You?"

Oh. My. God.

He's angry. The low whip of his voice has shivers running up my spine.

"I waited for you, you didn't come, so I, ah, I went to my car and drove home. I'm still in it—my car that is—at the apartment. I don't want to get out."

"Don't fucking move," he barks, and then the line goes dead.

Oh boy.

I don't move, not that I was planning on going anywhere. I wait until I see two headlights pull into the parking lot, and then hear the loud slam of a car door as Ace gets out and charges, not strides, right towards me. He's pissed. It's written all over his face. I know why. I moved when he told me not to. I shouldn't have done it, but I didn't think.

I unlock my car and climb out just as Ace reaches me.

"Apartment. Fucking now."

Oh man.

I nod and walk in front of him the whole way. When we reach my apartment, he shoves me slightly with his shoulder, using his set of keys to unlock the door and storm inside. He does a scour of the apartment while I just stand there, not really sure what I'm supposed to do or say. He's angry at me.

Maybe I should just keep my mouth shut.

"It's clear," he rumbles in his voice low. "Lock the doors, I have work to do tonight."

He's leaving me?

My heart slams to a stop and I whisper, "You're leaving me?"

His eyes flash to mine. "I have work to do."

"Ace, I'm sorry I didn't follow orders. You were

late, you didn't call or answer your phone, I thought I'd drive home. I didn't think it through. I'm sorry."

Those eyes are burning holes into mine. He's so angry, the muscle in his jaw keeps jumping. I've never seen him like this. Sure, I've not known him all that long, but I've still never seen him so aggravated. I know I did the wrong thing, but I'm okay, I'm here. Right? Surely there is no reason to be that angry.

"You didn't fucking think at all," he booms and I flinch, taking a step back.

"Why are you so angry?" I ask. "I know I screwed up. I won't do it again. I wasn't thinking at the time. I know I broke the rules but—"

"Rules?" he hisses. "You think I'm pissed because you broke the fucking rules and so stupidly walked off on your own?"

I nod. Because why else would he be pissed.

He shakes his head. "Your things were all over the ground."

My things were all over the ground? What . . . oh.

Oh. He thought I had been taken.

Ace thought I had been taken.

"Ace . . ."

"Don't," he growls, pinning me with another glare. "Just fucking don't."

It scared him. I can see it in his face. For a brief moment, he thought I'd been taken. He was afraid. My heart aches. I'm an idiot. An absolute idiot. Before I can say anything else, he turns and storms out of the apartment, slamming the door so loudly I flinch.

Dammit.

I fucked up. Bad.

I sit on the sofa for an hour.

I know there is an officer outside my door, I've heard him shuffling around and I even heard him speak to Ace at some point. I thought Ace might have come back, but he didn't. So I let him be. But it's eating away at me. I made a huge mistake, and worse, I upset Ace and that wasn't ever my intention. I didn't think what it would be like for him to see my things lying on the ground.

I can't sit here any longer. I need to go and see him, to apologize again. The last thing I ever wanted to do was scare him. That wasn't meant to happen, and I won't sleep tonight knowing he's next door angry, upset, and mostly hurt. I can't imagine how that would have felt, to see all my things strewn about on the floor and panicking that I had been taken.

I stand, straighten my clothes, walk over to my door, and open it. The officer guarding me is standing on the outside, leaning against the wall, staring blankly at nothing. What a boring job. I guess this is the part they all have to do at some point, even if they don't really want to. His eyes swing to me when I clear my throat, and he straightens. "What is it?"

"I'm going next door to see Ace. I just wanted to let you know."

He's already shaking his head. Why is he shaking his head?

"Ace has requested no visitors."

I don't think so.

"Look, I'm going over there, one way or another."

The officer raises his brows. "That's not going to happen."

"It is going to happen whether you like it or not. You can either walk me over there, or I'm going to scream this entire hall down. And trust me, I'm loud."

"I have a Taser," he warns.

I snort. "You Taser me, you're fired, and you know it."

He grumbles something under his breath, and then resigns himself to the fact that he is going to have to take me next door one way or another, and extends a hand. "Well, hurry up. If I get into trouble over this, you'll owe me."

I flash him my best smile. "I hear you. I'll tell him I forced you."

"Please, for the love of God, don't say that. I'd rather endure his wrath."

I giggle as I walk towards Ace's door. When I reach it, I knock three times and then step back and wait. It takes a few minutes, but finally the door swings open and Ace appears. His eyes flick to me, then to the officer behind me, and he growls, "I said no visitors."

"He had no choice," I say, crossing my arms. "Can I come in?"

"No."

He slams the door in my face. My mouth drops open and I start banging my fists on the door over and over. "I can do this all night, Ace!" I call. "Or I can try screaming, yelling, singing if I must . . ."

The door swings open again, this time Ace looks more than a little pissed off. "I'm busy. Can we do this tomorrow?"

"No," I say, stepping past him and walking into his apartment. "We do it now."

With an angry sigh, he closes the door after muttering something to the officer outside. He locks the door and turns to me. "I'm not in the mood, Hartley."

I cross my arms and stare at him. "I'm fully aware of that, Ace. But the fact of the matter is, I upset you earlier and I owe you an apology for it."

He doesn't say anything, he just stares at me, face blank.

"It's going to take a little more than that, huh?"

I exhale, rub my hands over my arms, and say, "Listen, I'm really sorry, okay? I mean that. I should have stayed at the restaurant. I shouldn't have gone off on my own. I can only imagine what it would have been like, you seeing all my stuff on the ground . . ."

"Are you done?"

Oh boy, he is really angry.

Now he's making me angry.

"If you're going to stand there and be a jerk, I won't bother saying sorry!" I snap, crossing my arms. "Honestly, Ace, I'm trying to do the right thing here, and you're just making it difficult—"

He takes a step towards me. I keep talking.

"I know I screwed up. I know and I'm trying to fix it."

Another step.

"But there is absolutely no need to be a jerk about it. Seriously. If you want to yell at me, go right ahead."

Another step. Oh God.

"Scream at me if you need to," I say, tilting my head back and looking up at him when he stops in front of me. "But don't treat me the way you are treating me right now."

"I want to scream at you," he growls, low.

"Okay."

"I want to fucking wring your neck for what you did."

Oh boy.

"I am so pissed."

God.

"So. Fucking. Pissed."

I swallow. "I know and—"

"You ever do something so incredibly stupid again . . . and I'll . . ."

He grinds his teeth together.

"Wring my neck?" I offer.

"Hartley?"

"Yes, Ace?"

"Shut the hell up."

With that, he takes another step forward, curls a hand around the back of my neck, and brings me in for a kiss. I'm in shock. For a moment I stand there, not completely sure I'm actually awake. Those lips, rough but soft, are moving over mine in a vigorous manner. My knees tremble, and I know I'm not dreaming. No. Definitely not.

Ace is kissing me.

Ace. Is. Kissing. Me.

Screw it. I might die tomorrow. Or the next day. Or sometime. I'm not going to waste a second longer. I reach up, twisting my fingers in his hair, and pull his head down closer so I can kiss him deeper. And kiss him deeper I do. I tangle my tongue with his, dragging a moan from his lips. One hand goes down around my waist and he hauls me up. My legs curl around his waist, and in two quick strides he has me on the sofa.

Down we go.

I whimper when his big body comes down over mine, grinding against me, those hot, hard muscles pressing against every part of me. It's been so long since I've felt a man so close, felt his mouth on mine, his body flush, his hands dragging over my skin. I close my eyes and let Ace deepen the kiss. We shouldn't be doing it, but neither of us are about to stop.

Ace's hand travels down my side, and curls around my thigh, pulling it up to hook around his waist. The short cotton pants I'm wearing are no barrier for the hard length rubbing against me. I whimper and arch into him, using the heel of my foot to push down on his ass, pressing him harder against my body. This earns me a low, deep growl, and he finally pulls his mouth away from mine.

"You drive me fuckin' crazy."

I stare at his lips, and already I want more. "I'm not sorry."

"I shouldn't be doing this."

I lean up, nipping his full lower lip. "Then stop."

He doesn't even think about that as he leans back, removing his shirt. He tosses it to the ground and rasps out, "Not going to happen."

All right then.

I'm not going to argue.

I stare as he hooks his thumbs into my shorts and slowly drags them down my legs. My cheeks flush when he drops them to the ground and his gaze rakes my naked lower half. I'm thankful I recently waxed, because I certainly wasn't planning on any man seeing me naked, so it's a damned miracle I thought to do it. Ace's jaw clenches as his eyes take in my exposed sex.

"You're wet," he murmurs, reaching down and dragging a finger through my sex, bringing it up and sliding it into his mouth.

Oh God.

That was hot.

"Fuck," he hisses, making light work of the rest of his clothes and mine.

My eyes travel down to the hard, jutting erection between his legs. Holy crap. It's as big and angry-looking as him. It's beautiful, swollen, ready. I lick my lips as he lowers himself over me, shifting just slightly to the side so his fingers can slip between my legs again. I gasp when he slides one inside, while using his thumb to stroke over my clit.

It feels amazing.

Nobody has touched me since Raymond, and I didn't realize just how much I've wanted it until this moment. My body is already wound up and ready to explode. I bite my bottom lip, trying to hold back, but my legs start shaking as my orgasm builds so fast I know it's going to be incredible.

"Stop holding onto it," Ace growls. "Let it go."

I exhale and a long, deep moan leaves my throat as I explode, having an orgasm for the first time in what feels like forever. Ace makes a pleased sound in his throat, stroking me a few more times, before slipping his fingers from my depths and moving his body over mine, nudging my legs wider apart with his big body.

His lips find mine, and I let him kiss me, long and deep. My fingers run up and down his back, my nails putting just enough pressure on his skin to earn me a pleased, slightly pained, groan. I run my foot up and down his calf, and then I drag my lips away from his and find his jaw, kissing the stubble there before lowering my mouth to his neck, where I nip him before sucking slightly.

"Fuck. Stop it," he pants. "I can only take so much."

Smiling against his skin, I reach my fingers back up and curl them into his hair, moving my mouth back against his and kissing him once more. He tastes incredible. His kisses go from deep, to frequent pecks, back to deep again. I'll take whatever I can get when it comes to him. As long as his lips are touching mine, I want it.

"Going to fuck you now," he murmurs.

"Okay," I whisper, my chest rising and falling with my pants.

He leans back, twists, and opens a drawer on the lamp table beside the couch. He jerks out a packet of condoms and pulls one out, tearing it open with his teeth and rolling it down that beautiful length. I don't think too much about the fact that he's got condoms beside his sofa, I just focus on him, and the anticipation building inside me.

When he falls back over me, his mouth drops and closes around one of my nipples. He sucks it into his mouth and gently nips at it. God. That feels incredible. I tighten my legs around his waist, needing him inside me. I don't care if that makes me seem desperate, because the fact of the matter is, I am. I need him, and I need him now.

"Ace, please," I mewl, pulling on his hair hard enough that I know it'll hurt a bit.

He shifts, and then the tip of him is pressing right there. God. Right there. I tilt my hips, edging him inside me. With a groan, he thrusts. One, hard thrust. He fills me, and a cry escapes my lips. Oh. My. God. A mix of pleasure and the most incredible kind of pain explodes in my body as it struggles to stretch around him, to accommodate his size after so long.

"Goddammit," he hisses. "Fuck."

He pulls his hips back slowly, and then drives back in. My cry turns into a whimper, as I ease around him. Only then do I feel it, really feel it. With every thrust, the pleasure builds inside of me, starting like a small fire inside my body, burning out until I'm crying out his name, until my nails are gliding down his back, until I don't think I can take it for a single second more.

"Ace," I gasp.

Nothing more needs to be said. His name is more than enough. His thrusting becomes more measured, perfectly timed strokes, rubbing over that bundle of nerves inside me, and before I know it, I'm arching for a final time, gasping out his name as I explode around him. Pulse after pulse of pleasure shakes my body, and my entire world feels like it stops spinning for one blissful moment.

It's just Ace and me.

"Fuck," Ace groans, and then his body shudders, too.

For a few moments, we lay there, both of us panting, both of us covered in a fine sheen of sweat. I run the tips of my fingers down Ace's arms, over the curve of his bicep, over his shoulders, and then slowly down his back. He's got his head nestled in the nook of my shoulder, and his breath tickles my neck. Slowly but surely it slows down, and he lifts off me, eyes holding mine. "You okay?"

Am I okay?

Dammit. That's sweet.

"Yeah," I say in a soft voice. "Are you?"

He nods, leaning down and pressing a kiss to my forehead before removing himself from me and discarding the condom. I sit up, pulling my clothes back on, and then I wait for him on the sofa while he cleans up in the bathroom. He comes out a few minutes later and sits down beside me. For a second, neither of us says anything, because honestly, I don't think we really know what to say.

It wasn't something I think either of us saw coming.

"Do you regret that?" I dare to say, looking over and meeting his eyes.

He shakes his head. "No."

"You're so quiet . . ."

He rubs a hand down his face, then drags it through his hair. "That's just . . . it's the first time since . . . Miranda."

Oh.

I get where he's coming from.

"For me, too."

His eyes widen slightly. "Really?"

"Yeah, really."

He doesn't say anything, he just stares at me with those penetrating eyes.

"Ace?"

"Mmmm?"

"Tell me about her."

TWENTY-ONE

"What was your life like with her?"

"Full," he tells me, his eyes swinging to mine. "She was an incredible woman."

I smile, loving the way his face lights up when he talks about her, the way the lines near his eyes soften, and his face seems to just relax. It's like she is a peaceful place for him, a place where he doesn't have to carry the weight of the world on his shoulders. I love that. I know what that feels like.

"What did you love the most about her?"

"Her laugh, she had a crazy laugh. It was kind of what drew me to her, you know? She was standing there, in a bar, head thrown back, laughing. I knew that I had to meet her, just to hear that laugh some more."

That's beautiful.

"Were you different before you lost her? Do you think losing her changed you?"

He thinks about that for a moment. "Yeah, absolutely. She used to tell me I was broody, so I guess

some things never change, but I was happier then. I
didn't feel anger, or regret, or this incredible sadness. I loved life."

"You don't love life now?" I ask him, understanding how that feels, to be stuck in sadness and unable
to find a way out. It took me a long time. His loss
is fresher than mine.

"I love my job, but there are times when I'm
alone, and I have nothing else. It's just me and my
job. It can be a lonely world."

Poor guy. I know how it feels to be surrounded
by people and yet feel completely alone. I can re-
late to that. I can understand it. I like understanding Ace, I like being able to respect his pain and know
exactly where it stems from. I think it connects us
on a level other people simply couldn't understand.

"What did you do for fun, before you lost Miranda? Surely there was something you enjoyed?"

He thinks about that, and then his eyes swing to
me. "I loved fishing. We used to go out most week-
ends, up to the mountains, to the lake, and we'd
fish and camp."

"Why don't you do that anymore?"

He shrugs. "Life got busy, never had time."

"I understand that," I admit. "I know how it feels.
Sometimes I'd rather stay cooped up, and never go
out. It seems easier to just forget life keeps going
on after you lose someone."

"Yeah," he murmurs.

"Tell me more about Miranda." I smile, studying
him. "I like hearing you talk about her."

Ace nods, those lips tipping up just a little at the
sides. God he'd be beautiful if he smiled. "She was
crazy. She kept me on my toes, that's for sure. I'll

never forget one time we were walking down the street and there were these dancers, two of them, trying to earn some money. There was a group of teenagers picking on this couple, and so Miranda kicked off her shoes and joined them, encouraging everyone watching to do the same. Soon enough, she had about a dozen people dancing, and laughing, and giving the couple money. She shut those teens up. She was good like that. She just had this edge about her, this light."

I smile. "It sounds like I would have liked her."

"You would have, because you're exactly the same."

I roll my eyes. "Come on, I wouldn't have danced in public with a group of strangers just to get back at a group of rude, bitchy teenagers."

Ace snorts. "Yeah, you would."

"I can't believe she did that."

"That's the kind of person she was. She always wanted to make people laugh, and if she couldn't make them laugh, she'd just annoy the ever lovin' hell out of them."

"Good for her, there aren't enough people left like that in this world. People who just stick it to the man and do what they feel is right."

Ace agrees with a low "Hmmm," then continues, "She was special, that's for sure. She would have traveled the world and put a smile on everyone's face if she had half the chance."

I smile at him.

"What about you?" he asks, changing the subject. "What kind of man was Raymond?"

"He was sweet," I tell him. "Sweet as hell. He did little things every day to make me smile. He would leave a note, or just turn the washing machine on with a load of clothes—anything to make my life easier. He was always trying to make me happy."

"Not many men left like that in the world," Ace murmurs.

"No, there aren't. I was lucky. I *am* lucky. I got to experience the very best kind, even if it was for such a short time."

"Me too."

"Do you think you'll ever love anyone again?" I ask him, and his eyes flash, true emotion showing through for a second.

"I don't know. It's hard to think anyone could compare," he tells me in a low tone. "But I don't believe there is only one person for everyone out there, either. I think it's possible to love again. It might not be the same, but that doesn't mean it won't be just as good."

I nod thoughtfully. I agree with him.

"Do *you* think it's possible?" he asks me.

"Yeah, of course. I mean, no love is the same, but I think everyone has more than one, without a doubt."

"Mmmm," he murmurs, staring at my lips.

"You're staring at me," I laugh softly. "How the tables have turned."

"That's because you're beautiful."

I flush and rub my hands together. "And to think I didn't like you when we first met."

He shakes his head, those lips twitching again. "Not many people do."

"You said you've always been like that. Did it get worse after you lost Miranda?"

He nods. "I didn't cope all that well, and instead

of dealing with it, I just shut down. It was hard to get myself out of that place. It became . . . second nature so to speak."

"So you weren't angry when you were with her?"

"No," he tells me. "Broody yes, angry no."

"Do you think you'll ever feel good enough to let that anger go?"

He studies me. "I hope so."

"What was it like," I dare to ask, "knowing you were going to lose her? I think all the time if I just had the chance to say good bye to Raymond, it might have hurt less, but I don't believe that anymore."

His face grows a little sad. "Honestly, by the time she passed, I almost wanted it for her. Watching her suffer, watching the pain, watching her smile even when it hurt, knowing she was doing that for me, it killed me. It wasn't just losing her, that was hell of course, but it was watching her suffer slowly first."

I nod, swallowing the thick lump in my throat. "I can imagine. I don't think I could have coped, knowing it was such a long, painful process."

"It wasn't easy, but I did get to say good bye to her. I can't imagine how hard it would have been for you not to."

I nod, looking down. "It was horrible, but I have the good memories. I wasn't there. I didn't see it. I can keep Raymond in a safe place in my heart. You had to watch Miranda fade, and that takes strength."

He stares at me. "I guess we are both stronger than we think."

"I guess we are."

His mouth quirks a little bit again.

"You know what I think, Detective?"

"What do you think, Hartley?"

"I think you'd stop the world for just a second if you smiled."

His eyes flash with something unfamiliar to me, and for a moment, I think he might just smile, but he doesn't.

He will, one day. I'll make sure of that.

"Have you heard anything from Jacob?" he asks me, changing the subject.

I grin at him.

"Stop grinning at me, I'm just asking a question."

"Anyone would think you're jealous, Detective."

"I don't get jealous," he says, his voice dropping low. "I was just asking."

"Nobody ever 'just asks,' and you know it. Just come out and say what you have to say."

He crosses those big arms. "I don't like that dickhead, not one single bit. I don't understand what you saw in him."

"Jacob was a nice guy, he just wasn't boyfriend material."

"No, he was girlfriend material."

I giggle. "Gosh, getting a bit cranky there, aren't we?"

Ace grunts.

"Anyway, we're just friends. You don't need to concern yourself over it."

He gets up from his spot on the sofa. "Wasn't concerned."

He leans down, brushing his lips across my forehead as he passes.

"You tell yourself whatever you have to," I call when he straightens and goes into the kitchen.

"Will a cup of tea stop you from talking?"

I laugh.

He shakes his head, those eyes dancing.

"Yes, please," I answer, unable to wipe the grin off my face.

"Wipe the smirk, Hartley."

I can't, but I know he doesn't mind.

Not really.

It's the first time I've felt good in . . . forever.

T: Come over and stay at my house tonight. I
   want to see you.

I stare down at the text message from Taylor just as I reach my apartment after finishing up a twelve-hour training shift at the hospital, where I got to watch my first baby being born. It was incredible. Definitely makes it worthwhile. I'm exhausted, and Ace is busy with work tonight, so maybe going and hanging out with Taylor might be a good thing.

H: I just finished up a shift at the hospital.
   Weren't you working tonight?
T: No. I'm not on. Come over. I miss you.

I could use a girls' night.

H: Let me tell Ace. I'll get back to you.
T: Okay!

I dial Ace's number while locking my apartment door. The cop on the other side gives me a nod. I hate closing the door right in his face, it makes me feel rude, but Ace has assured me, more than once, that it's normal and they're used to it. Still, I feel bad.

"Hart," Ace answers, his voice smooth and calm.

"Hey," I say softly. "Listen, how safe is it for me to go to Taylor's house for the night?"

"Safe enough, so long as we keep the watch on outside and you ensure that Taylor locks all her doors."

"She's in a third-floor apartment, I think we're fairly safe so long as someone is at the main entrance."

Ace makes his *hmmmm* sound of agreement, then says, "Yeah, that's good."

"So it's okay for me to go?"

"Yeah, go. Will do you good."

I snort. "You sound like my father or something."

He grunts. "Believe me, the thoughts I've been having about you today are anything but fatherly."

I flush. "Is that right?"

"It's right," he murmurs, low and sexy.

"It's a shame you're working then."

"A fuckin' shame."

I squirm, wishing more than anything that he wasn't working tonight.

"Oh well, I guess you have your thoughts to keep you company, then."

He growls, and I could swear my panties pack up and run away from me. "You better go to your friend's house, or I'll have to walk away from this case so I can come home and feel myself inside you again. And I don't have time for that, unfortunately, because the sooner I can find this fucker and remove him from your life, the better."

I agree softly, but even I can hear the husky edge to my voice. "Okay, big guy."

"Get Bill outside to escort you over to Taylor's,

and I'll give him a call and tell him to wait outside there for the night, too."

"Okay. Thank you."

"Give me a call before you go to sleep tonight, let me know you're safe."

My heart swells. "Okay, detective."

"Okay, darlin'. Good night."

Darlin'.

Swoon.

"Good night."

I hang up the phone and quickly text Taylor back.

H: I'm on my way!
T: Yay! I'll have the essentials ready.

I rush into my room, change into a pair of jeans and a tank, and then pack some things I'll need for the night before heading back out into the kitchen. I check around quickly to make sure I've got everything, and then I step out into the hall, locking the door behind me. Bill is already waiting, and when he sees me, he says, "Ready to go?"

I nod, happy I'm finally doing something seminormal for a change. It's been a while since I've gone out and just had some fun with Taylor. The last few weeks have been a roller coaster of emotion and fear and pain. This is the first time I feel okay. I don't know how long that'll last, so I'm going to hang on with both hands and pray it doesn't leave.

The drive to Taylor's takes about ten minutes. Riding in the cop car with these guys never gets old. I have a smile on my face the entire journey. When we arrive at Taylor's, I look up to her apartment and see her standing in the window. I can't see her face from here, but she gives me a wave.

"Did you want to come in and check?" I ask Bill. He looks up at Taylor. "That your friend?"

"Yeah, that's her."

"That's all good, then. I'll walk you to the door, but she is clearly not in any danger."

I smile and slide out of the cop car, letting my eyes scan the streets automatically before I move quickly to the front door. Bill follows close behind me, doing the same. When I reach the lift, he rides with me up to the third floor. He checks the halls, and then turns to me, "It's all good. I'll be down at the front entrance, I'll make sure nobody comes up without going past me."

"Thank you, Bill," I smile. "Have a good night."

He nods as the doors to the elevator close. I walk to Taylor's door and knock. A minute passes, and then I hear the lock unclick and the door open. Taylor stands in the doorway, but she's not the happy person I'd swear was just waving to me from the window. Of course, I couldn't see her face, but now . . . she looks terrified. Something cold washes over me, and her lips part to say something, to warn me maybe, but it's too late.

A figure steps out from behind her. I can tell it's a man right away because of his height, and also the lean build with enough muscle to tell me it is definitely not a woman.

I can't see his face, he's wearing a full-faced mask with only eyes and nose holes. He's also wearing a pair of shades, so I can't see the shape or even the color of his eyes. He's holding a massive butcher knife in one hand, and a gun in the other. That gun points directly at the back of my best friend's head. My entire world stops moving. I can't breathe. I can't think. I can't do anything but stand there and stare.

"Get inside."

His voice is muffled by some sort of voice changer that is over his mouth, somehow connected behind his head, maybe by a strap, so it comes out sounding crackly and machinelike.

I take a shaky step forward, my knees trembling, my body cold from head to toe. I should scream, or turn and run, or call out to someone, but I can't do that. I can't because I know he will pull the trigger of the gun that's aimed at Taylor's head. I will not allow that to happen. So I go inside, just like he demands.

"Stand over there, hands on your head," he orders, pointing the gun at Taylor and nodding in the direction of the kitchen. "Or I scatter her brains."

I flinch and do as he says, walking over to where the kitchen is. My bag drops to the ground as I put my hands up above my head. Taylor is shoved next to me and we both stand there like that, watching as he shuts and locks the door. Then he turns and faces us. His head tips down to my handbag, and he demands, "Kick that to me."

I do as he says, kicking the bag across the room. He reaches down, emptying the contents on the ground. He flicks through my things, and then looks up at me. I might not be able to see his eyes, but he terrifies me. He's dressed all in black, from head to toe, not an inch of skin to be seen. Black gloves over his fingers, black boots over his feet, and black clothing covers his body. The mask he's wearing is low enough to touch the top of his shirt.

All black.

That's all I can see.

"Where's your cell phone?" he demands.

No.

Dammit.

No.

I reach into my pocket with shaky fingers and pull it out, wishing I had Ace on speed dial, or I thought to try and send a text, something. If he takes this phone, it's all over. There will be no way Ace will know I'm gone. He thinks I'm safe at Taylor's. He steps forward and snatches the phone from my hand, unlocking it then doing something—his gloved fingers press at the screen, but he can't seem to achieve whatever it is he's trying to do.

He walks closer to me. "Send the cop a message. Tell him you're safe."

No.

"And if you send anything else, I'll kill her."

Taylor looks at me, and she's terrified. Her eyes are wide and bloodshot, her body is trembling, and her mouth is agape and frightened. I will not let him hurt her. So I do as he says.

H: I'm at Taylor's. I'm safe. Have a good night.

I turn the screen to him, and he nods sharply. I press SEND and he snatches the phone from my hand, turning it off and shoving it into his pocket. I study him, trying to figure out if I know him from the way he moves, the way he acts, but I can't pick up anything familiar. He's tall, but with those clothes on, it's hard to know much more. They're almost bulky in their appearance, making it hard to fully see his build. All I know for certain is that this man is the killer, and he was clever enough to get hold of me using my best friend.

I can't let him hurt Taylor.

I have to figure out a way to get us both out of here.

TWENTY-TWO

I blink awake and, for a moment, I'm dazed and confused. I don't remember being knocked out, or falling asleep, but by the bouncing around I can feel, I know I've been out for a while. We're in a car, or a truck, maybe a van. I go to reach up and rub my eyes, but my hands are cuffed in front of me. Panic sets in as I remember the man who was at Taylor's house.

Taylor.

I jerk my head to the left, and then to the right. We're in a van, that much is obvious due to the size of the back and the white walls. Taylor is to my right, hands cuffed in front of her, too, her eyes wide and alarmed, focused on me. How did she get roped into this? I was praying he would let her go, but he hasn't. He hasn't and now she's here. We're here, *together*.

"Are you okay?" I whisper, my eyes going to the front of the car where the man in black is driving.

There is a massive screen sectioning us from him,

and by the looks of it, it wouldn't smash easily. Outside of that, there is nothing else in the back of the van except Taylor and me, and the blanket we've been placed down on. The back doors are padlocked together, to ensure we can't jump out. Our hands and feet are cuffed. We're stuck.

"I'm scared, Hartley," she whispers.

My chest twists, and my whole body prickles. Yes, I'm afraid too. I feel the same fear coursing through my body. "Me too. We're going to get out of here, though. There are two of us, and only one of him. We'll figure it out."

Do I even believe the words coming out of my mouth?

This feels like a dream. Almost like it can't be happening, and we'll wake up any moment.

Only I know we won't.

"I d-d-didn't want to text you," she squeaks. "I didn't, but he made me. I was so afraid. He just showed up at my door and demanded I contact you and get you over to my house. It worked. He made me stand by the window and wave when you arrived, so the police officer wouldn't be concerned."

A genius plan, really.

"How did he get us out of the apartment?" I wonder out loud.

"Through an emergency exit. I was still awake. He drugged you. I had to lead him out while he carried you. He told me if I made even a sound, he'd shoot you right in front of me." She hiccups. "He had a van parked in the alley."

Fuck.

The tricky bastard.

"Do you know who he is?" I ask her.

She shakes her head. "No, I can't tell anything, he's so covered up. I did figure something out, though, when he was mumbling to himself."

I nod, encouraging her. "What?"

"He was saying something about how he would break you. I didn't know what he was talking about, but he kept mumbling something about Raymond, and how it wasn't working because of that stupid 'cop' and how he was going to use me to do the job."

My heart feels like it's come to a complete stop. He's going to try and use Taylor to break me, to finish his sick little game. My skin prickles and vomit rises in my throat. It makes perfect sense. He wasn't getting what he wanted out of using Raymond, because we figured it out, so now he's going for the only other person who truly matters to me—my best friend. I have to think. I can't break. Not now. But I can't let him hurt my friend, either. Dammit. My mind spins as I try to figure out a way we can get out of this.

But I will find a way. I need to pull on my big girl panties, push my fear aside, and get through this. I will get through this. No matter what. Taylor was my rock when Raymond died, she was there for me during my weakest moments, now it's my turn to give that back to her.

"Hartley," she croaks. "Do you think he's going to hurt me?"

"No," I say, my voice stern. "No. I won't allow that to happen. I'll figure something out, Taylor. I will."

"I don't want to die," she says as a tear slides down her cheek.

I shuffle closer to her, reaching out as best I can so one of my fingers skims hers. "I won't let that happen. I will get us out of this. I don't know how I'll do that, but I will. Whoever this sicko is, he won't win, Tay. I promise."

"He's clever. Everything he has done has been precise. He has gotten not just one, but two of us away from a police watch."

I'm terrified, right down to my bones, because I know she's right, but I don't let that show. I'm in this situation now. I can either retreat into myself like I used to when the pain of Ray's death was too much to bear, or I can face whatever is going to meet us at the other end and fight. Regardless, I know I'm not getting out of this unscathed, so I'd rather go down fighting.

"I know, believe me I know, but everyone has a weakness, Taylor. Even him. I'll find it."

"What if you don't get the chance? What if he just takes us out there and kills us and—"

"Listen to me," I say, my voice steady. "He isn't going to do that. This entire thing, it's a game to him. A massive game. He won't just end it without achieving what he wants."

She nods, biting her lower lip. I know how she feels inside right now. I've been feeling the same fear for the past month. It's a deep-lodged fear that you can't make rational sense of, no matter how hard you try. Taylor is terrified, but she's feeling just the beginning of that terror. I've lived with it for long enough that I'm a lot more focused.

He thought he could break me and wear me down. He did the opposite.

Because I won't go down without a fight.

The man, who I have decided to call Black, original I know, takes us to an old, run-down house in the middle of nowhere. Thick trees surround us, seeming to go on for miles and miles, with a house perched in the middle of a small clearing. In its day, I imagine it was grand. Three stories high, old white paint peeling from the thick wood rafters. A big wraparound deck that was once beautiful but now just looks unkempt and makes the entire house look creepy.

Taylor and I have been ordered out of the van, and are standing with our backs to it, the gun pointed towards us, as we watch Black, who has still not revealed himself. I want to see his face. I want to know what kind of person is so sick and twisted in the mind that they can do something like this.

I stand as close to Taylor as possible, not wanting to leave her side for a single second. I don't know what's awaiting us in there, but I know that I'm not going to let him hurt her. He's going to try and use her, and I have to figure out a way to stop that from happening.

It's become his mission to break me.

How can I stop him from doing that, while keeping Taylor safe at the same time?

If I act as if I don't care, he's going to go to extremes to prove I do. He's not stupid and he'll know it's an act. If I give him the reaction he wants . . . will that be enough to stop him? Can I act? Can I make him truly believe I'm weak-willed and broken, just to get him to stay away from my best friend? And if I do, will he hurt her even when she's no longer of use to him?

My heart pounds.

My mind spins.

I don't know what I should do. All I know is I have to do something. Taking a deep breath, I make a choice. I'm not entirely sure it's the right one, but at this point I can only hope that it'll take the attention off Taylor and keep me safe. I stare at Black, and in my best shaky voice I say, "I don't know who you are, but please don't hurt my friend."

I sound weak.

Pathetic even.

The masked head turns in my direction, and in that muffled voice he says, "Walk."

I glance at Taylor, and she's biting her lip so hard I can see blood pooling to the surface. She's terrified, probably trying to talk herself out of doing something stupid. I know how she feels, but with our ankles and hands cuffed, we can't even make a run for it. We can only shuffle, little bits at a time. There is no way we could escape him right now, even if we wanted to.

"Towards the house. Make one wrong move, I start shooting your friend in different places until you get to watch her bleed to death."

"Please don't," I croak, and even I believe the weak tone to my voice. "She hasn't done anything wrong."

"Walk," he growls again, pointing the gun in Taylor's direction.

My heart hammers, but I do as he says, I walk.

For a second, it feels like two big hands curl around my heart and squeeze, because what if we don't get out alive? How many people actually get out of these situations? I haven't read many stories where they escape from them. No.

We shuffle up the steps with great difficulty, falling more than once and having a gun shoved into the back of our heads to hurry us up. We get to the top and shuffle across the dusty, wooden porch until we reach the front door. With the gun pointed on us, Black opens it and hisses "Inside' in our general direction. We both enter. The house is old and all of the furniture is covered in white sheets, as if nobody has lived here for a long time.

We're shoved down a dusty hall, and I cough more than once as we stir up the dust that has settled on the floor. There is a faint track worn down the middle of the hallway, showing someone's been here before, probably him. We reach a room and he kicks the door open. Once we're both inside, I see that it's fully secured—barred windows, no furniture to use for weapons, and a keypad locked door have my heart sinking.

This isn't good.

"I'll be back to start with you soon," Black says to me, and even though I can't see anything, I'm sure his eyes are zeroed in on me. I can feel them burning a hole into mine.

I hold back my shiver.

He steps out, slamming the door. The *beep beep* of it locking lets us know we are fully alone with no way out. I turn to Taylor and she finally lets the tears flow freely, rolling down her cheeks. She smothers a sob with her bound hands, and I want to hug her. I want to go over and tell her it's going to be okay, to give her something, anything that'll make her feel better.

But I don't even know if I believe it myself.

Are we going to get out of this? Will Ace have even figured out I'm gone? What if he hasn't? Even if he does, what if he can't find us? He hasn't managed to crack the Bowtie Killer case yet, how is he supposed to do it in a matter of days, or less?

My heart sinks and a feeling of dread washes over me.

What if we don't get out of here?

TWENTY-THREE

Ace

"What do you mean you didn't go and check Taylor's apartment?" I roar at Bill, pacing the room.

"She was in the window, she waved. I walked Hartley into the building, I even took the elevator up with her, I just didn't actually go into the apartment. I didn't know anyone was there, Ace. If I did, I wouldn't have let her in."

"It was your job to check!" I bellow.

Bill glances down at the floor, and I know I'm being too hard on him. I know it. He was doing his job. The bastard who took Hartley and Taylor did a good job of making it look like everything was safe and well at Taylor's house. When no one could get ahold of either of them, we went straight there and found them gone. There was nothing there but their phones, and Hartley's purse.

Hartley was gone.

Both girls were gone.

That fucker has both of them.

"Ace," my boss, Craig, says, putting a hand on my shoulder, "calm down. We're going to find them."

"We haven't been able to find any of the others!" I growl, running a hand down my face.

"We also didn't know back then what we know now. We're going to find them. We have every detective working on all the information as we speak."

"I've been over all of it. Fuck, I must have missed something. There has to be some clue, somewhere."

"If there is, we'll find it."

My shoulders tense up as I try to go over everything that's happened, racking my brain to figure out what I might have missed. There has to be something. Fuck. My mind goes to Hartley and Taylor. How long will he hold them before he kills them? Will he kill Taylor, because she is of no use to him? What would that do to Hartley? My chest tightens at the thought. She'd go to the ends of the earth for her best friend. If he hurts Taylor, it'll destroy Hart.

Maybe that's why he has the both of them. Maybe he's going to use Taylor to get to Hartley, because his sick little plan hasn't worked so far.

Fuck.

I think of the girl I've grown a soft spot for in the last few weeks. Her stubborn, yet gentle attitude has grown on me and she's gotten closer to me than any other woman since my wife. There is something about her, something spectacular and strong, something kind and sweet. She's a strange mix, and I can't get her out of my head.

I like her.

A fucking lot.

And I told her I'd protect her.

"We need to think here, Ace," Craig says. "Tell me if there is anything in those notes we haven't looked into. Something Hartley has said, something you haven't looked into."

I think, going through all our conversations in my head. One stands out.

"Hartley said she went to a support group after she lost her husband. She had an idea once that maybe this killer was finding women there, knowing they are fragile. Shit, I was supposed to look into that but I forgot. Can we get all the numbers for the support groups in the area?"

"I'll get someone on it right away. Is there anything else? Anything at all?"

I shake my head, because I can't fucking think right now.

I can't imagine losing her.

Hartley.

"Do you keep a record of the people who have come to your support sessions?" I say to Diana, the woman who runs a support group closest to Hartley's place. There are only two in the area, and no one at the other one has ever seen Hartley or heard her name.

"Yes, we do."

"I'll need to know if you've ever had any of these people," I say, sliding her a piece of paper with all the victims' names.

She glances down at it, and her brows go up. "Yes, yes I recognize two of those names. I'd have to check through records for the rest—we have a lot of people come through here and I'm not familiar with all of them."

Bingo.

Hartley was right.

Smart girl. Fuck, why didn't I listen to her?

"Which names do you recognize?" I ask.

She points to Hartley's name, and to Georgia's. "Those two. I remember them quite well. I saw Georgia had . . . passed recently. It was devastating."

"Yes, I can't go into too much detail, but I believe Hartley is in danger. I'm going to need any information you can give me, any at all."

"Of course, Detective. I have photos taken from the support group events, and I have transcripts, things like that."

"Give me everything you have," I say, my voice tight even though I'm not intending it to be. "Are you able to do that for me now?"

"Absolutely. Take a seat."

I sit down on an old, plastic chair beside a magazine rack, and stare at the pale wooden floor. I can't get the anxious feeling out of my chest. If I don't make it in time, if I don't find this fucker, I'm going to lose her. I'm going to lose her, and I can't . . . I can't lose someone else. Not again. A strange tightening in my chest tells me I'm far fonder of the girl than I've allowed myself to believe. That scares me. But what scares me more is not being able to explore that.

I told her I'd keep her safe. I promised. I should have been with her every fucking second. This man, I knew he was tricky, I knew he was good. I've been on this case long enough to know that, and I let her out of my sight. Why the fuck did I trust someone else to do a job I should have been doing? If I was doing it, she might still be here.

"Fuck," I whisper to myself, running a hand through my hair.

"Here you are," Diana says, coming back out with a few folders. She hands them to me and I go directly to the one labeled WATSON, HARTLEY.

"I also found files on the other two girls on your list—it turns out they've been here too. Do I need to be concerned, Detective?"

"I'll let you know," I murmur, too focused on the file.

I go through the transcripts, basically just Hartley describing how she's been feeling, how the group has been helping her, things like that. Some groups keep them, others don't. I flick past the pages and stop at a stack of photos. I start flicking through them, my eyes zoning in on Hartley in different scenarios, sometimes talking in a group, other times doing activities with them.

She looks empty.

Her eyes look so sad.

I remember staring at myself in the mirror and seeing that same pain.

I hand the photos to Diana as I continue to flick through them, studying all the people in them, seeing if any stand out. So far, nobody does. I can get Diana to give me the names of every person in these photos, but it'll take a long fucking time to get through them all for questioning.

I'm on the second to last photo when I see it.

In the background there is half a face, glancing around a doorframe. It's a man, that's for certain, and he's staring in at the group, holding a mop in his hand, wearing what seems to be a pair of coveralls. I squint and bring the photo closer. There is something familiar about him, but it's hard to tell because he's a little blurry.

"This man, who is he?" I ask Diana.

She glances at the photo.

And when she says the name, my blood runs cold.

No.

Fuck.

No.

TWENTY-FOUR

Hartley

Black doesn't come back in for the entire night.

I don't know what he's doing. I don't want to know. I'm simply grateful for the fact that every second he stays out there, we have a better chance of surviving. Taylor fell asleep within the first hour, after exhausting herself from crying. I sat on the ground, and let her rest her head on my lap, and only when she was asleep, did I let my fear break loose. I let the warm, salty tears run down my cheeks, but I don't let them beat me.

I can feel the fear, but I don't have to give in to it.

My legs are numb, my body aches, and I'm already getting hungry. It's well into the night, maybe early morning, I'm not sure. It's dark. I can't see. I can't hear anything. The only thing that comes through in the darkness is my shallow breathing and the occasional shuffling sounds from above. I can't hear Taylor, but she shifts around in my lap every now and then, so I know she's still okay. For now.

My mind twists and I try to think of a way to get

us out of this. It doesn't matter which way I play it, my best option is to act like he's broken me. At the very least, he'll leave Taylor alone. If I act tough, he is guaranteed to torment her. I have to take the risk in putting on a show and hoping it'll make him forget about using her. I only hope that doesn't mean he feels her place is no longer needed. Either way, it's a risk. This risk is the one I'm going with, because it makes more sense.

He wants to break me.

It's what he's doing this for.

I want to see his face. I want to see the man behind the mask. I want to know who decided my life was worth destroying with his sick game. I want to know if he's random, or if I know him. I want answers. And the longer I sit here, the more frustrated and frightened I become. I think about Ace, and I wonder if he's figured it out yet. And if he has, how does he feel? Is he scared?

Then I wonder if I'll ever see him again, and that brings a tightening into my chest I haven't felt since Raymond. A tightening I can feel right to my very core, a deep affection I didn't realize I had developed. The thought of not seeing Ace again, the thought of him worrying where we are, and feeling like he's failed, makes me want to scream. I know how he'll take this. He'll blame himself. Then he'll blame me, because he'll be angry, and scared, but after that, he'll feel the fear.

And I don't want him to feel that fear.

The door makes a clicking sound and my head jerks up. A moment later, it swings open and a light flicks on. I squint and Taylor jerks upright with a gasp. It takes me a solid few minutes to be able to see anything, but when my eyes adjust, I see Black reaching the bottom of the stairs, a machete in one hand, a chain in the other. He's fully masked. Still covered all in black. That doesn't matter. My eyes zone in on his hands, and the items he's holding.

I feel like I'm going to pass out from the fear that invades my body in that very moment.

"Get up," he orders in that hoarse voice. "Now."

Taylor and I get to our feet, but it takes all my strength to stay on them as my knees begin to tremble. I try to ignore Taylor's whimper beside me, as I keep all my focus on Black.

"I'm sure you're wondering by now, who I am, and why I chose you," he says, running his fingers over the chain in his right hand. "Those answers will all come in time, but they will only come at the right moment. I don't want to answer those questions for you, I want you to answer them for yourselves."

"I know what you want from me," I say, and I don't have to put on much of a show to get my voice shaky, because it's already mostly there. "Leave my friend out of this. Please."

His head swivels in my direction. "And what is it I want with you, Hartley?"

"You picked me for a reason," I say, my voice trembling. "You did your research to torment me the way you did. Taylor has nothing to do with this."

"Always the hero," he says. "So strong."

Strong.

God.

I need him to think I'm weak. That he's won.

"But I will break you, and that's what your little

friend here is for," he rattles the chain in Taylor's direction.

No.

"Leave her alone," I cry, once again. It isn't an act. The thought of him hurting Taylor sends shivers up my spine and causes a coldness to take over my whole body. I let a lone tear roll down my cheek. "Don't hurt her. Please. I'm begging you."

He swings the chain in Taylor's direction, causing her to take a little jump back and lose her footing, falling onto her back with a cry. She has no way to stop her fall, so she lands hard.

"Please!" I cry, shuffling forward. "Please stop. Don't hurt her. I'll do anything. Just don't."

It isn't hard for me to cry, and a month of pent-up fear flows out and I let it, not even attempting to hold it back. If he needs me to break to leave her be, then that's what he'll get. I won't let him hurt her. If I have to play this until I'm on the ground sobbing and begging for mercy, I will do it. I will do whatever it takes. I sob, staring at the masked man, praying this works. "Dammit. What more do you want from me? You've tormented me enough. Just do what you have to do with me, but leave her alone. I'm begging you."

He looks at me, and for a long moment, he just stares. I wonder if beneath that mask he has his eyes narrowed, studying me. Just when I think he's taking it all in, believing my act, he throws his head back and . . . laughs.

My body goes straight and my tears instantly stop flowing. When he looks back at me, I know his eyes are pinned to mine even though I can't see anything. "How stupid do you think I am? Honestly,

Hartley. I've watched you for long enough to know you're not that weak—to think you actually believed I'd fall for that. Good plan, though. Trying to pretend for the sake of your friend. It isn't going to work."

He's onto me? Just like that. How?

"I'll do whatever you want, just don't hurt her," I try again, desperately.

He laughs again.

"Please," I beg, lowering down onto my knees. Shame flooding my cheeks. Because deep down, I know he's right. I'm not this weak. But for Taylor, I'll do anything. I'll be anything. "Please, don't hurt her."

"Get off your knees!" he orders. "Your act won't fly with me. I don't need to hurt her to break you. That would be too easy, and too cliché. Don't you think?"

I look up at him, still on my knees. By the way he says the next words, I can almost hear him smiling beneath that mask. "I simply need to hurt you."

I'm confused, and for a moment, I just stare. Hurt me? Isn't that the plan all along? To hurt me? By using my husband, and now Taylor? I don't understand.

"There is more than one way to skin a cat, Hartley. Of course you'd put on a show to protect your friend from getting hurt. And, granted, I could hurt her enough to break you, but you're anticipating that, and like I said before, cliché. I like to play by a different set of rules. No. If you think you're so tough, so unbreakable, then I'll let *her* watch *you* suffer. You see, I don't need to lay a finger on her to traumatize and ruin her for the rest of her life, in which case, ruining the person you hold dearest."

Taylor makes a pained sound on the ground beside me. She's stayed quiet. She's not stupid. But those words scare her. I know they do. Taylor is soft at heart. She might be full of sass, but she's a gentle person. Seeing someone get hurt . . . will destroy her. He's right about that.

My skin prickles. The smart bastard. "Just let her go. Please. She isn't part of this."

It's pathetic. I know it even as the words are coming out of my mouth, but I can't stop them. I have to try, once more. I can't let my best friend watch me get hurt, I know what it'll do to her. Vomit rises in my throat, and I look over at her. She's as pale as a ghost, staring at Black.

He laughs again. "Oh, but Hartley. She is."

Then he swings the chain. It hits me across the face so hard my head splits. Blood spurts out from a wound in my forehead. I can feel the skin split apart. Pain, unlike any I've ever felt, tears through my skull and I stumble, falling to the ground, screaming in agony. Not even the strongest person could handle that. Taylor's screams fill the small room and she begs, "Please, please stop. Please don't hurt her."

The chain swings again, like a whip, the clatter filling the space until the end connects with my shoulder. I tumble backwards and another pained scream rips from my throat. Tears pool in my eyes, mixing with the blood running down my face.

"Stop!" Taylor screams. "Stop!"

Hearing her agonized cries rips me in two. It tears into my very soul. He knows it—it's precisely why he's doing it. But he will not break me. I'll take every beating under the sun before I let him break me. But God, it hurts so bad. So damned bad. I have to fight with everything I am inside to stop myself from breaking.

"Taylor, close your eyes," I yell at my friend. "Close them. And trust me."

"Hartley," she wails.

"Close them!"

I don't know if she does, all I hear is his evil laugh muffled by that voice changer. I turn to face him, pushing to my hands and knees and panting through the pain, "You will not fucking win. Beat me until I'm dead, but you will not break me. She might not like to see this, but she will recover. I, however, will not give in to you. So beat me until there is nothing left. Cut me into a thousand tiny pieces. Do whatever it is your weak, pathetic ass has to do. But. You. Will. Not. Win. You know nothing about me. There isn't a single damned thing you could do that would make me yield to you."

"Is that so?" he says, raising his hand.

I prepare for another blow.

But he takes off his mask.

I stare.

For a moment, that's all I can do. Just stare. My entire body feels funny, tingly even, like I must be seeing it wrong, like maybe this is a dream after all. I mean, it has to be. It has to be a dream. It can't be real. It simply cannot be real. Even through the blood soaking my vision, and the pain pounding in my head, I can see him clearly enough. And I heard Taylor's gasp. I heard it as clearly as I heard my own.

But it still doesn't seem real.

But there he is, standing in front of me.

Jacob.

Jacob, who was sweet, romantic, kind.

Jacob, who took me out and kissed me when I was sad.

Jacob, who changed my locks so I wouldn't feel afraid.

Jacob, who I would have sworn on my life was a good and loyal man.

"Broken now?"

His voice hits me right in the heart, like a deadly whip.

I dated a serial killer. I kissed and let a serial killer into my home and into my life. I confided in him. I trusted him. I dated a man who had killed not one, not two, but three women. And I, Hartley Watson, was stupid enough to let him into my life, and nearly into my heart.

I'm numb.

I can't stop staring at him.

It feels like my body is going to just go out from beneath me.

"Cat got your tongue?" He laughs, stepping forward, looking down at me. "Imagine how Raymond would feel looking down on you right now? His wife, his dear sweet wife, dating a killer."

I can't breathe.

"She let him into their home, into her life, and she had no idea. None. He'd be rolling in his grave if he could see how stupid you've been. If he could see the woman he left behind was locking lips with a man who has, if I might say so with pride, had plenty of blood on his hands."

I'm going to be sick.

I vomit, there isn't much more in my body to come out, except blood and mucus, but I vomit. I vomit until I'm dry retching and gagging. Tears run down my face, my nose dribbles. This must be a nightmare. It has to be. It can't be him.

"You think you're so smart. You think you can't be broken, but guess what?" He kneels down in front of me and I stare into the eyes that I would have told anyone who asked, were kind and loving. "You just broke."

My whole body starts shaking.

I let him into my apartment. He could have hurt anyone, because of me. Ace. Lena . . . Oh God. I fell right into his trap. All along he was right there, and I dove in headfirst. Now that I look at it, it's almost glaringly obvious, but at the time I would have sworn to anyone that Jacob was a good man.

Oh God.

"You were easier than I thought, honestly. With the cop living next door, I worried he might catch on, but like the stupid fools you both are, you let me slip right past your radar. And don't get me started on the cop. He questioned me. Twice. But instead of actually asking me questions that would've probably given him a clue, he was too caught up in trying to make me look like a nobody. He wanted you and he couldn't look past that to see the truth. Idiot."

My throat closes and I can barely breathe as he continues.

"All along I was there, right in front of you, and you didn't see it. I knew I'd break you, but I must admit I didn't think it would be me that did the deed. I tried your husband, but you overcame that; I tried your best friend, but still you wouldn't crack; and then it came to me . . . it came to me and I knew. I knew exactly what it was that would destroy you."

He leans closer and chuckles.

"It was *me*. It was simply knowing that you let me into your world, and your friends' worlds, and how close I was the entire time . . . that's all it took. And now look at you—pathetic, broken, on the floor with nothing. You're exactly where I want you, Hartley. Now the real fun can begin."

A strangled sob climbs up my throat and escapes. Jacob. Sweet, kind Jacob. This has to be a joke. It has to be.

"I will say," he continues, as if he's having a general conversation with just anyone, "I didn't think I'd involve myself, let my face be shown, until you. I tormented those other girls, by doing very similar things to you, but I never became a part of their lives. I watched you for so long, and I knew you were going to change the rules, there was just something about you—so stubborn, so strong. I needed to challenge myself, to make the stakes higher. At first I didn't know how to get close to you, but when I saw you on that dating website, I knew what I had to do."

Taylor makes a pained sound, and I know what she's thinking.

She's thinking this is her fault. But it isn't. He said he's been watching me, which means he would have found a way to get to me, no matter what.

"Do you want to know the first place I saw you?" he says, rocking back on his heels, keeping that machete close to his body. "It was one of those support groups. I found the other girls at those, too. Easy pickings. I noticed you right away, and I knew you were different. You want to know how?"

I don't.

I don't.

"You rolled your eyes," he chuckles. "You rolled your eyes when someone said something—oh, I can't remember what it was, but all I could think was, she's the one. Even in her time of grief, when her face is so empty because she's so hurt, she's got an edge. I needed a challenge. You became my challenge."

My vision blurs, and my head pounds.

"I knew you were never going to be the same. You simply couldn't be."

I can't speak. I cannot speak.

"Of course I imagined the final kill, when I carve a bowtie into your neck. You'd be my trophy, my greatest achievement. Mommy would be so proud. She'd be so proud of me."

What the hell?

I glance at him and he's staring blankly at the wall. *Mommy?* What does his mother have to do with this? Did she torment him as a child? Did she drag out his suffering? Why a bowtie? So many questions flood my mind, but are quickly replaced with horror when I realize how close he was all along.

He was right there.

"Anyway, I'm getting ahead of myself," he continues, breaking himself out of whatever twisted memory was playing in his head. "I'm quite looking forward to listening to you beg for your life.

And you will beg, Hartley. I will kill you knowing I'm the man that broke you."

"No you won't!"

Taylor's voice whips through the air and my head spins just in time to see her lunge at Jacob. In his storytelling and his focus on me, he'd forgotten all about her. She hits him hard and both of them tumble backwards. For a moment, I am frozen in shock, but then I move, as quickly as I can, pushing past the pain and the horror. Taylor lands on top of Jacob and they roll for a few seconds, all the while she's slamming her cuffed hands down over and over onto his face.

Jacob raises the machete, and drives it into her leg.

Blood pours to the surface as Taylor's screams fill the room. He pulls it out and raises it again, aiming higher this time—for her throat.

He's going to kill her.

No.

This is my opportunity. Taylor gave me an opening, and I'm going to take it. With all my might, I lunge forward. I hit Jacob in the back and he stumbles forward, the machete flying from his hand and skittering across the room. He spins around as I raise my cuffed hands, and I hit him as hard as I can across the face. A loud crunch feels the room, and warm blood splatters over me as his nose starts bleeding. Then I move quickly, going for the machete.

I shuffle towards it, but he's quicker and lunges forward, his hand curling around into my hair and jerking me backwards. I lose my footing and land with a thud. I roll to my back just as he's leaning down to lift me up. I shove my legs into his body, sending him across the room again with the force of my kick. I'm panting as I push to my feet. He makes a pained sound, and I glance at the door. I have to move.

So I stand and I hop. I hop as fast as I can towards the stairs, and then I use my cuffed hands to hold the railing and I hop with all my might, step by step, up into the house. I hop down the hall, my body aching, my lungs screaming from exertion. I reach the kitchen, eyes darting around. It takes Jacob a few minutes to get to his feet, but he makes it out into the kitchen just as I start shuffling through the drawers.

He stops and stares at me, machete in his hand, grin on his bloodied face.

"You didn't think you were going to get away that easily, did you?"

TWENTY-FIVE

Ace

I can't believe it's Jacob. When I heard his name, I didn't want to believe it. When I looked at the picture, I still didn't want to believe it. Even when he pulled his mask off, I found it hard to believe. But no matter how I try to deny it, the truth is right in front of me. All along it has been right in front of me. Fucking right there.

"Jacob," I growl. "Fucking Jacob. I should have known. I felt it in my gut that there was something wrong with that man, but I ignored it. I ignored it. If I had listened, I would have figured it out."

"No time to blame yourself, Henderson," Craig says. "We need to find this man."

"What have we managed to dig up on him so far, now that we know it's him?"

Caleb, another detective, says, "Obviously, his first name is Jacob, but his last name is different. He started using a fake last name when he started hunting for girls. I've looked into his real name, he was adopted as a baby. Single mother. She's dead, I'm looking into her."

"Anything else we can work with?" Craig says. "Do we know where the mother lived? Perhaps he's in the same house?"

"Got someone on that now," I say, running a hand through my hair, trying to fight back the anger at myself. He was right there in front of me the whole fucking time.

"How did he find her on a fuckin' dating app?" Caleb grunts, crossing his tattooed arms over his chest.

I exhale for calm. "He knew enough about her from the support group, maybe he followed her, tapped into her phone, even listened to Taylor and got the idea as a way to get into her life. I can't see him coming up with that—he waited too long, my guess is he found out about Taylor setting her up and used it as an opening to get into her life."

"He must be savvy with technology, then," Caleb mutters. "It ain't easy to get the information he's gotten, or tap into people's computers . . ."

"People do it all the time," I mutter. "That's what's fuckin' wrong with the world, it's too easy to find out what you want to know, if you're good with computers."

"Yeah," Caleb grunts. "Do we know how he found out so much about Hartley's husband? How he found out all those things?"

"The smart fucker started breaking into her apartment when the locks were flimsy," I growl. "Then, when she got scared, he changed them and must've kept a key. That's why it was only after I changed them again that it stopped happening inside her house, and he started sending things to her instead."

"So all the things he used to torment her, he found in her apartment? The clever, sick fuck."

I nod sharply. "Hartley said she kept boxes of her husband's things. It wouldn't have taken much for him to snoop through them and learn enough to torment her. Then there's the fact the dirty fuck was dating her, so I'm sure she told him things."

"Smart man, involving himself in her life and even helping her when she got scared. He thought it through," Craig murmurs.

"He's a fucking dead man if I get hold of him."

"He was right there, the whole fuckin' time," Caleb says out loud, but it's more to himself. "Just dating her . . . right there, under our noses."

I know what he means. The idea that he was right there, right fucking there. I hate it. I study Caleb, and give him a nod. He's good at his job. He's working closely on a few murder cases, and he has a knack for it. I spent some time with him going over them, getting tips and pointers. He's a couple of years younger than me, but the man has an edge that even I wouldn't want to cross. He has had a hard past—I don't know much about it but I know he hasn't had it easy.

It makes him incredible at his job. A determined, strong worker who doesn't take any crap. He lives and breathes his job. He doesn't have a family or even a woman, which surprises me. He's got the looks that stop most females in their tracks—a dark, dangerous edge. He'll make something out of himself, that's for sure, and when he does he'll take the world by storm. I'm glad to have him on the team right now.

"It's a good tactic," I growl, getting back to the subject. "He was squeaky clean, he did a good job of changing his name and living a clean life. He checked out."

"We have his name now, so we're going to find something," Craig assures me.

"What if it's too fuckin' late?"

Both men look at me.

"We'll find her," Craig assures me again.

"Ace," another officer says, coming into the room. "I have some information on the mother. I found a few records. I don't know much about his life with her, but I found a photo. Have a look."

He hands me an old photo and a few notes he's made. I look down to see a junkie-looking blonde standing beside a little boy. She's got her hand possessively on his shoulder, but it's what he's wearing that my eyes zone in on. A bowtie. He's wearing a bowtie.

God.

"How did a woman like this adopt a child?" I growl.

"She was probably not like that when she adopted. Drugs do bad things to people," Craig explains. "She obviously tormented the boy."

My throat gets tight, but I don't focus on the feeling long. I go through the notes and come across an address.

"This her old house?"

"Yes," the officer tells me. "It's about four hours away, but I think it's worth checking out. There is a high chance he's taken them there."

He's right.

I stand. "Let's find this fucker, and end him."

TWENTY-SIX

Hartley

The drawers are empty. Every single one of them.

There are no knives, or anything else that could be used as a weapon, anywhere.

The smart bastard thought of everything.

Jacob's laugh fills my space. "Gosh, I mean I thought you were a little smarter than this, but to run into the kitchen? Did you really think there would be a big butcher knife waiting on the table, so you could kill me and skip off into the sunset? This isn't a movie, Hartley."

My knees tremble. He's on the other side of the counter, that massive blade in his hand. My head is pounding. My body hurts. I feel like I'm going to pass out. But right now, I'm out of that room. This will be the only chance I have of ever getting out of here. I have to think. Taylor is down there, bleeding. She could die if I don't get this right.

God. Taylor. Is it already too late? There was so much blood. She tried to save me, she tried to save me and she got hurt. I have to get us out of here.

There isn't much I can do with my hands and feet bound.

"There is nowhere for you to go, Hartley," he chuckles, running a thumb down the edge of the knife, looking completely deranged with his bloodied face.

I cannot believe I let this man into my life.

I shake that thought.

Focus.

"No matter which way you try to escape, I will catch you, and I will slit your throat."

My knees are shaking, my hands are sweating, but I don't move.

There has to be a way.

There just has to be.

"What did you honestly think would happen if you ran from me? Do you think you'd actually be able to kill me?"

He laughs.

"We both know you wouldn't," he continues. "You might be strong, Hartley, but you don't have it in you to take a life."

Something moves behind him, and my eyes dart to it. Taylor is shuffling down the hall. For a moment, I think I'm seeing things. But it's her. My brave, beautiful friend. Looking like she may just die, but she's doing it. She has blood pouring from the wound in her leg, but she's moving steadily. For now.

He hasn't heard her. He hasn't seen her. He screwed up. They always screw up, even if it's so tiny no one notices. No one can be that perfect. And he just left his door wide open. In chasing me, he forgot about Taylor. He assumed she was too injured to move, or maybe dead, or maybe in his rush to come after me he simply forgot about her.

But he screwed up.

And now here she is, coming down the hall behind him, hands clenched in front of her, determination shining through her pain.

I have to keep him distracted. This is literally our only chance.

"I could," I say, meeting his eyes. "Kill you."

He laughs again, swinging the machete around. "What would Raymond think of his beautiful wife doing such a thing? He'd be horrified."

That won't work. I know Raymond would much rather me rid the world of someone like Jacob than allow him to take my life and then go on to take others. "He'd be glad I rid the world of one more piece of scum."

Jacob's face tightens, just a bit. I know I'm winding him up. That's the point. I want him angry. Mostly, I want him distracted.

"You're so worried about what my dead husband would think of me," I say, shifting just slightly to the left so I can see Taylor without having to look directly at her. "What would your mother think of you? I mean, you're obviously doing this for her, right? Imagine if she saw you now, letting a victim escape. I'm embarrassed for you."

Red floods his cheeks and something incredibly terrifying passes over his eyes. It's an evil that runs deep. Scarring that is imprinted on his very soul. He's damaged. Severely damaged. How did I never notice that in his eyes before? After all, they are the window to the soul. I missed the worst part of him.

"For that," he hisses, "I'll slit your throat twice."

"Go ahead, I'll be dead after the first one."

His jaw tics.

"You think you can break me, Jacob, but you're forgetting one thing . . ."

Taylor is right behind him. She is ready. I'm ready. Together we're going to get out of this. We're going to, I won't let it end any other way.

"You have to be breakable to be broken," I say, my voice steely. "And in case you haven't noticed, I'm made out of the strongest steel. You were never going to break me. Take that one to Mommy."

Taylor raises her hands, and she hits him as hard as she can with her bound fists, using the cuffs to add force to her blow. She hits him so hard, he falls forward, the machete tumbling from his hands. He goes down to his knees, clearly dazed, and she hits him again, raising her arms above her head, then slamming them down on his. "Nobody hurts my best friend," she croaks, her voice so weak, yet so incredibly strong. "No one."

Jacob's hands go out in front of him, and he grabs the machete, spinning around. He swings at Taylor, but misses. I have to act fast. My eyes scan the kitchen, and in the corner, sitting on top of some towels, I see an old meat tenderizer, made of pure, solid steel, used for hitting meat over and over until it's tender. I don't even want to know why he left that out, but it's the only thing I can see. I rush over and pick it up, just as Jacob lands on Taylor, the two of them crashing to the ground. He raises the machete, hissing, "I'll kill you for that, you little—"

I don't think.

I just swing.

I swing with every single ounce of strength I have left in my body.

I smash Jacob in the back of the head, and he goes crashing down, a loud crack ringing out, a crunch I'm not sure I'll ever forget. Then he slumps to the side, blood pooling around his head, eyes open. The machete tumbles from his hand. Taylor lies on her back, panting, her eyes on me.

I killed him.

My knees give out and I drop to the ground, staring at the man with lifeless eyes, laying on the floor. The man who tried to take my life. My best friend's life. The man who took too many lives. I just killed him.

Taylor makes a groaning sound, and I look over to her. There is too much blood on her leg. The strain has made it worse, and it's pooling far too heavily now.

I glance back at Jacob once more, then I look back to my best friend. I take a deep, shaky breath, and push to my knees.

I'm not that easily broken.

Taylor and I, we're strong. Unbreakable. We always have been.

It's time we got out of here.

So on shaky feet, with shaky hands, I shuffle over to where he is laid out, kneel down beside him, and find the keys to the cuffs, which are in his pocket along with seven or eight others. I heard them jingling when he was moving around. I shuffle over to Taylor and uncuff her, then, using my teeth, I uncuff my hands as well.

Then, I take a deep, shaky breath and lean down to lift up my best friend.

It's my turn to save her now.
And save her, I will.
The monster is gone.
It's all over.

TWENTY-SEVEN

"Come on, honey," I say to Taylor, pulling her along with me. Her arm is slung over my shoulder and we're both exhausted. All I want to do right now is sleep for the next week, but I have to get us both to safety. I have to. And I will.

He's gone.

He's gone, but neither of us knows where we are. We could be anywhere. I don't even know if we're in the same city, let alone the same state. But I know my friend needs a doctor. Urgently. The deep gash on her leg is bleeding too heavily. My entire body aches, and carrying her weight is draining every last piece of energy from me.

One foot in front of the other.

We trudge through the mud, and it makes a squelching sound as we move through the trees. It's impossible to avoid the rain that's been falling for the last two hours. I can't stop. I'd love to stop, to let us both rest, but if we stop now I know she won't make it. I've wrapped her leg again as tightly as I can, but that'll only hold for so long before she'll start slipping away.

"Stay awake for me, Tay," I say to her, my voice croaky. "Stay awake. If you go to sleep, you'll die. Do you understand me?"

"I understand," she croaks, but her voice is so flat, so broken, it terrifies me.

"Just keep focusing on one step at a time. One foot in front of the other, we're going to get you out of here."

I can't see any sign of light, or hear any sound of traffic. For all I know, we could be walking deeper and deeper into the forest surrounding Jacob's hidden house. I shiver at the horror we left behind. He's gone—by my hand—and that thought alone puts an angry ache on my heart I'd much rather forget. I don't even want to think about what happened back there.

I just have to keep reminding myself he's gone.

My mind wanders as we walk, and I try to ignore the throbbing pain in my leg from the deep knife wound and the pounding in my skull. There is so much dried blood on me, I can feel it stuck to my face, cracking when I move, itching. I can't reach up and scratch at it, because it'll start bleeding again. I know I've already bled quite enough, because my shirt is soaked with it.

I think about Jacob. I still can't wrap my mind around it. I still cannot forget the shocked feeling in my chest when he pulled that full-face mask off to reveal a man I dated, a man who was kind to me, a man I trusted, a man I let into my home and into my life.

Now I look back, the signs were there. He was

clever, smart even. He was never going to make those signs too obvious, but he did present them.

Taking me to the restaurant where Raymond and I got married, making me feel at times like I was paranoid and losing my mind, changing the locks on my apartment, and no further break-ins after Ace replaced those. It all makes sense now, like it was so incredibly obvious.

Jacob.

My heart clenches, and I fight back an exhausted sob. I would have never believed for a single second that the human mind would be capable of being so utterly sick and twisted, but he has proved to me that you can stand in the presence of what seems like an angel, only to find out that beneath the surface is the ugliest, deadliest demon you've ever encountered. Jacob's act was flawless. It was perfection.

He had us all fooled.

Even Ace.

"My leg hurts," Taylor whimpers, her weight getting heavier and heavier with each step.

"I know, honey," I whisper, trying to will my knees not to buckle, because I need them to stay up and get us to safety. "Just a little further."

"Can we stop?" she pleads in a voice far too weak for my liking. "Can we just stop and sleep? It's dark. I want to stop."

"We can't stop," I whisper, trying to keep my body from falling. "We have to keep going."

I take a shaky breath and keep dragging her through the trees, pulling us along for hours on end, until I honestly don't know how I'm still managing to move my feet. One foot in front of the other—I repeat this over and over in my head, it's on constant. Just keep moving. If I stop, we're going to die. That alone is enough for me to battle through the ache, through the pain, through the agony.

My feet have gone numb, my knees burn with every step, sending sharp pains up my thighs. My back is on fire and my shoulders are tight from holding Taylor's weight. I'm fighting back vomit, and my head is pounding so hard, I'm sure my vision would be blurred if I was sitting in the light. But I keep moving. I just keep pulling us along.

"L-L-Lights."

I wonder if I'm hearing her correctly, because I could swear Taylor just said "lights." I look up, and I'm right—my vision is blurred. I can't see much, in fact, I'm fairly certain I can't see anything at all. Exhaustion has finally taken its toll on my body.

"What?" I whisper.

"Blue . . . red . . . lights. I can see them."

Blue and red? Like police?

I focus ahead, but I still can't see anything. My head is spinning, I'm starting to wonder if my head injury is worse than I thought.

"Where, Taylor?" I order in a soft, weak tone.

"Str-Straight ahead."

Is she imagining it? Is she so far gone she's picturing an escape? Freedom? I don't know, I'm too afraid to hope, but I keep walking anyway, moving in a straight line, dodging the trees where I can and trying to keep us headed towards the lights she keeps telling me she can see more clearly as we near.

"Police," she cries happily. "It's police!"

My knees start buckling as finally I can see very faint red and blue flashing lights. They're closer than

I think, I know because I can hear voices now, too. My vision isn't what it should be, but Taylor is right, they're real. With one last deep breath into my lungs, I use the last of my strength to pull her forward, getting closer and closer by the second until finally I feel the road beneath my feet.

"What the—"

That's the last thing I hear before we both collapse. I don't feel a thing as I land on the ground—exhaustion, pain, fear, terror, it all consumes my body. Everything I've been keeping in for the last few days finally takes over. I fall in and out of consciousness. Frantic voices are all around us, and a hard set of arms curls around me. A face is in my hair, and I hear a hushed voice murmuring, "Oh God. Hartley. Baby. I've got you. You're safe. I've got you. Fuck, I'm so sorry."

Is that Ace? I don't know. I know it feels good. So good. Warm. Safe. Now I know he's here, now I know he's got me and I'm free, I slip into peaceful nothingness. I finally let it flood my body. I stop holding it back. I stop fighting it. I just let it in. I've been praying for it, every second since Jacob got hold of us.

Bliss.

Pure bliss.

Blinding lights are the first thing I notice when I come to. I reach up and rub my eyes, wincing as a sharp pain travels through my skull. My head is bandaged, and for a moment, I'm confused and dazed. Where the hell am I? What's happening? I rub at my eyes again, getting frustrated when I can't seem to clear my vision correctly. These stupid bandages.

"Stop rubbing at that, you're all bandaged up."

A feminine voice travels into my ears and I try to focus on it. It's only then I realize one of my eyes is patched. With the uncovered one, I zone in on the woman standing beside me. I'm in a hospital. As I wake, the beeping machines beside me become more obvious, and suddenly, it sounds very loud in here. I look at the blonde nurse, who is smiling down at me. "Hi there."

One blink.

Then another.

"What . . . what?"

"You're in the hospital. You've been out for a couple of days. Do you remember anything?"

Jacob.

Taylor.

"Taylor." I croak.

"Taylor is well. She had surgery on her leg, but she's recovering just fine. She's safe. As are you."

Safe.

Safe.

"Ace?" I whisper, my vision becoming clearer by the second.

"Detective Henderson has requested to be called the second you wake. I'll have someone notify him."

I nod, rubbing at my throat. "Water?"

She hands me a cup of water and I sip at it. It relieves my throat instantly. I swallow half the cup, then hand it back to her. "The doctor will be in shortly. I'll just check your vitals and then we'll let you know what has happened."

I nod and stare around the room as she checks my vitals and fills out my chart. An older gentleman comes in a minute later, wearing scrubs. I'm guessing he's the doctor.

"Ah, Dr. Henry. She's up."

The doctor comes in and stops by my bed, looking down at me. "Hi there, Hartley, how are you feeling?"

"Like I've been hit by a train," I admit.

He laughs softly. "I imagine. I'll let you know what procedures you've had, get you up to scratch. You had a lot of bumps and bruises, and you were severely dehydrated, so we made sure that was the first thing we took care of. The cut on your head was deep, it took eight stitches, and the swelling behind it was quite severe, but we're keeping an eye on it. The wound was very close to your eye, and there was some severe swelling there, too. We had to operate to reduce that, but your vision shouldn't be affected in any way. We've also stitched the deep gash on your leg. However, it was directly in muscle, so you were very lucky. Other than that, a lot of rest and fluids is all you'll need."

I nod. "Thank you."

Lucky.

I don't know if I'd call us lucky. Although, we did escape the hands of a serial killer.

That has to count for something.

"Hart?"

My good eye darts to the door, and Ace is standing in it, filling its narrow frame. Tears well in my eyes as I stare at him and take in his broken expression, and the pain he's flicking in my direction.

"We'll leave you to it," the doctor says as he leaves with the nurse.

"Hey, big guy," I say, but my bottom lip is trembling.

Ace walks over, leans down, and circles those big arms around me, pulling me into him in a way that makes me feel like I'm coming home. His hug is full of affection, and relief, and so much more. His face nuzzles into my neck and his body engulfs mine. He was afraid. I know he was afraid. He didn't find me. Couldn't. I can't even begin to fathom what went through his head for those terrifying moments of his life.

"I couldn't fucking find you," he says, pulling back and cupping my chin in one of his big hands. "But . . . I found him through the support group you told me about. You were right, he was watching girls from there all along, playing the role of a janitor so he could get information. If I had looked into that earlier . . ."

"It wouldn't have mattered what you did, he would have found a way," I say softly. "He was smart. It's what made him so good. But I'm here. I'm alive. And he's gone."

"I'm so fucking sorry. I should have taken you to Taylor's house . . ."

"Don't," I say, reaching up and cupping his jaw. "This was something he would have found a way to do, no matter what and you know that."

"Are you okay after experiencing what you did? I know firsthand that it can mess with your head . . ."

I shake my head, giving him a tired smile. "He wasn't going to win, Ace. I wasn't going to let that happen. So outside of these superficial injuries on the outside, he didn't touch the inside."

I take his hand and press it over my heart.

"You're incredibly fuckin' brave. I saw what happened out there. I saw him. What you both did."

I swallow and take a shaky breath. "Jacob."

Ace's jaw ticks. "He was right there the whole time, under our noses. It's always someone close."

"You couldn't have known. I didn't even know. He was good, Ace. He had everything mapped out, perfectly planned."

Ace nods, stiffly, but he does nod. "He's gone now, because of you both. You did that. You got yourself and Taylor out, and then you walked over ten miles injured, carrying your friend. You're the most incredible woman I've ever met in my entire fucking life."

"I could say the same about you, big guy." I smile weakly. "Hey, Ace?"

He looks at me.

"Why do you think he did it? Did you find out much about him?"

Ace studies me. "We're still looking, but from what we could tell about the woman who raised him, she was abusive. Possibly physically and sexually. In the few pictures we dug up, she looked very overpowering."

"He said something about her when I was in there, about her being proud."

"A lot of the times, killers do have someone they're trying to make proud of them. It could be that she abused him, made him feel worthless and pathetic. He wanted to prove to her that he wasn't. He wanted to show her he was strong. He did that in the form of manipulation and violence. In one of the photos, he was wearing a bowtie."

"Oh," I say, my chest clenching. "I guess that makes sense why he had that particular style. Still, if she was so cruel to him, so horrible, why would he want to be the same?"

"His mind isn't like yours and mine, sweetheart. It's twisted. He had the mind of a sociopath. The cool demeanor he kept, the way he involved himself in your life, that takes skill but it also takes serious lack of emotion. That's how those kinds of people get to others. They tell wild tales, they make themselves out to be amazing people. They can manipulate anyone. They're the most dangerous kind."

"I shiver when I think of the depths he went to, to get to me. The research, the careful skill . . ."

"He's gone now," Ace says kindly, his voice low. "He's gone."

"Why do you think he picked women who had lost someone?"

"Losing his mother was his trigger. He was probably feeling the same emotions, only in a twisted, more deranged kind of way. He targeted what he was feeling. He went for people who were alone, and sad, and broken, just like him. He tormented them, probably in ways he was tormented. Perhaps the woman who adopted him tormented him about the loss of someone in his family. It always connects back."

I think about it, and as much as I'm glad the world has one less crazy out there, I feel bad that Jacob lived that kind of life. The kind of life that led him to do such horrible things. What was his childhood like for him to lose his mind so completely? It makes sense, now that I know more about his story, and I guess I'll never know what went on in the depths of his brain, but I imagine it was a very traumatized place.

I wonder if he's at peace now? Maybe that's how it was supposed to go for him. To switch off the demons.

I shudder.

"Thanks for telling me all that, it . . . helps," I whisper.

"Anything for you," he murmurs.

I smile over at him, so grateful he came into my life. So damned grateful.

He leans down, brushing his lips across mine. "You're changing everything for me, Hartley Watson."

I kiss him back, softly. "You've already changed everything for me, Ace Henderson."

And I wouldn't have it any other way.

TWENTY-EIGHT

"Stop fussing, Hartley," Taylor groans, slapping my hand away as I try to pull yet another blanket over her. "I'm not a cripple, you know."

I roll my eyes, reaching for the blanket again, but she slaps it away.

"Stop fighting me, will you?" I snap at her. "You've got a serious leg injury, the least you can let me do is cover you up and keep you warm."

"I can pull my own blanket up."

I give her a look. "Taylor, you're three seconds away from getting a swift kick to the shin."

She pokes a tongue out at me, takes the blanket, and jerks it up her body. "Are you happy now?"

"Not really," I mutter, eyeing the food on the coffee table beside the sofa.

"I'm not hungry."

I cross my arms. "Well I'm not leaving until you eat that, so it's your choice."

She makes a frustrated sound, but takes the banana I lift off the tray and hand to her. Her leg is in a full-length cast. The doctors had to operate—there was ligament damage, as well as bone damage and a major loss of blood. She's going to be off it for at least six weeks, and she's less than impressed about it. Other than that, she fared well, as did I.

Outside of cuts and bruises, and dehydration, we are probably the two luckiest girls in the world, because we escaped the hands of a well-known serial killer in one piece. And we did it together. So she can yell profanities at me as much as she wants, and fuss and carry on, I'm not leaving her side because she didn't leave mine. We're in this together.

"I liked you so much better when you were just my best friend, not my nurse," she grumbles between mouthfuls.

"I see the patient is still complaining?"

I look over my shoulder to see Ace walking into my apartment where Taylor will be staying for a few weeks until she's able to move around on her own. He's got a brown paper bag in one hand, two coffees in the other. He looks at Taylor, and she scowls at him, before her eyes drop to the bag. "If there's muffins in there, you might just be allowed closer."

He gives her a look, and then thrusts the bag at me. "Two double chocolate, two lattes."

"You're amazing." I smile at him, and then turn to Taylor. "Are you going to stop snapping like a rabid dog so we can share these muffins?"

She huffs but nods, and I sit down at the end of the couch where there is just enough of a gap for me to squeeze my bottom in. I pull out a muffin and hand it to her, and she discards the banana with a quick toss back onto the coffee table. Ace sits down on the sofa across from us, his eyes on mine.

"How are you feeling?"

My eye is still sore and patched up, and the stitches in my head are bugging me, but otherwise I feel good. Really good. I'm alive. I lived in fear for weeks, and then the days we were in Jacob's clutches . . . I have been given a second chance and I certainly am not going to waste it.

"I feel good, I'm still tired, but I'm good."

"She's obviously not that tired, she's going to start offering to wipe my butt soon!" Taylor grumbles between mouthfuls.

Ace snorts. "Well, you do owe it to her."

Taylor rolls her eyes, but smiles at me. She's lucky I love her.

"We've closed the case, informed the other victims' families about Jacob, so they can finally get closure too," Ace tells me.

My heart breaks for those three girls who didn't get the second chance Taylor and I got.

"How did their families take it?" I ask.

Taylor directs her eyes to Ace, listening in.

"They didn't take it great, but as I said, they got their closure, and because of that, they can finally start moving on with their lives as best they can."

I nod. Understanding. It doesn't bring anyone back, but at least now they don't have to live in fear that there is still someone out there, planning his next hunt, finding his next victim.

"I'm glad they can finally get peace."

Ace nods. "As can you."

I exhale and smile. "Yeah. I'm not wasting this second chance. I can't say the same for Taylor. She's going to get pushed off the nearest balcony if she keeps it up."

She flips me off. "You try being an invalid, with no leg."

"You have a leg, it's just out of action," I inform her.

"Same difference."

"You're alive, Taylor, don't forget that," Ace says, his voice firm, but kind.

She looks to him, scowling, and after a few seconds she exhales and murmurs, "Yes, I know. I'm sorry."

"Not everyone gets a second chance to make their life better, take it for what it is and don't waste it."

She ponders this, as do I.

Raymond, Miranda, and those three girls Jacob took before Taylor and me. None of them got a second chance. Their lives were cut short. This is our chance to do something good. To make something of ourselves. To change the world, if that's what we need. An idea pops into my mind, and my eyes swing to Ace.

"I have an idea."

His brows go up. "I'm listening."

"It's not much, but what if we created something, say a website, where people could come and share their stories of second chances? Be it survival of an illness, recovery from an accident, anything where they have beaten the odds and come out of something alive. I know that when I was afraid, it felt like there was nowhere I could find comfort. I felt like there was no way I'd ever feel okay again."

"That's a great idea," Taylor says, perking up. "Every time you look for something on the internet, all you find are the horror stories, about death, and pain, and heartache. What about if there was a place you could find stories of encouragement, of survival, of miracles and second chances. We could even set it up so people could search stories similar to what they're going through."

"Yes!" I cry happily. "Like if they've been given bad news about cancer, and want to read how someone has overcome it."

"Or if they've been told they'll never walk again, or have a serious injury . . ." Taylor cries throwing her hands up. "It'll be a place where they can find positive experiences, things to help them get through."

"I think you girls are onto something," Ace says, looking at me with those eyes again.

The ones that say he adores me.

The ones that say he's proud of me.

My heart swells.

"We can add Raymond's story, and Miranda's, and even what happened with Jacob as a start. Then we can categorize it all, so people suffering with grief and pain can find stories of how it can get better, of how there is always a light at the end of the tunnel."

"It's perfect," I beam at her.

"It's more than perfect, it'll change the world. I'm going to get started, right now. I know some amazing website designers. Quickly, get my laptop."

I hand her the laptop, and I grab a pen and paper.

And we get to work on changing the world.

One step at a time.

"You're so fucking perfect," Ace murmurs, running his nose up the side of my neck until he meets my jaw. He kisses it softly, before tangling his fingers into my hair, turning my face to the side, and finding my lips.

My fingers glide up his arms, over his biceps, and settle on his shoulders. My legs wrap firmly around his hips, and I kiss him deep, loving how he tastes, loving how he feels, loving every single thing about him. I never thought I'd meet anyone after Raymond who could spark life in my soul, I never thought I'd feel it again, but I have. Ace is showing me that there are second chances, not just at life and recovery, but at love.

Ace is my second chance.

"More," I whimper when his tongue laps at mine, teasing me, taunting me.

"You want more?" he growls.

"Yes," I breathe.

He pulls his mouth from mine, sliding down my body until his face is between my legs. He nudges my knees apart, looking up at me with those hooded eyes, before dipping his head and capturing my clit with his mouth. I gasp and thrust upwards, heels digging into the comforter, as his mouth devours me with long, tantalizing licks and fast, powerful thrusts.

"Ace," I cry out, fingers holding the blanket so hard they ache. "Oh God."

He works his tongue in fluid movements, building me right up to the edge, before sliding two fin-

gers inside me. I explode, crying his name, thrashing
around beneath him, my thighs capturing his head
as he sucks every last shudder from my body. He
pulls his mouth away and looks at me with hungry
eyes. I want him as much as he wants me, possibly
more.

"I need you," I order in a hoarse tone. "Right
now."

He takes hold of my hips, and with one effortless move, launches me up and takes me with him
as his back hits the bed and my body comes over
his. My knees straddle him, my hands land on his
chest, and I look into those incredible eyes, wanting this possibly more than I've ever wanted anything in my life.

"Fuck me, slow," he growls, lifting my hips and
reaching between us, taking his cock in his hand
and guiding it to my entrance.

I slowly lower myself down onto him, letting
him fill me, letting him stretch me. A gasp leaves my
lips and my head tips back as I sink onto him, my
body exploding with pleasure as I start to rock, a
slow motion of my hips that quickly turns into
more frantic jerks. Ace growls, fingers digging into
the flesh of my bottom, and I know it won't be long
for me.

It feels so good.

My fingernails slide down his chest as I rock
harder, faster, my breasts bouncing, my hair falling
down my back, my mouth open and little pants
leaving my throat. It builds quickly, starting as a
slow burn from the inside before exploding out like
a volcano. I scream out Ace's name as what is probably the best orgasm I've ever had rocks my body.

I nearly miss his growls of satisfaction as he thrusts his hips upwards to meet my rocking, as well as his ragged cry as his releases fill the room.

I fall forward, hands not strong enough to hold me up. My cheek presses against his slightly sweaty chest, and he immediately curls his fingers into my hair, tugging my head back gently so he can capture my mouth in another kiss. He tastes like me, and like sex, and like Ace. It's incredible. I nuzzle against him, slowing my breathing, loving the way his big body feels around mine.

"I'm real proud of you, honey," he rasps into the silence.

I keep my cheek on his chest when I answer, "You are?"

"Yeah, I am. What you and Taylor are doing. It's incredible. It'll help so many people out there, who have nowhere else to turn."

"I hope so," I whisper.

"It will. You've taken the best of a bad situation, and turned it into something you can share with the world. Not many people can say they have that kind of determination or strength. You could have crumbled, but you came out stronger."

I squeeze his sides. "I couldn't have done any of it without you. You're the reason I fought when he had us, you're the reason I believed there was a chance I could escape. You kept me strong, even in my darkest moments, Ace. I don't know what I would have done without you."

He goes silent, and I know he's pondering my words.

"Even though," I continue. "There were times I wanted to fly-kick you in the face for being such a jerk. And honestly, those manners of yours . . . terrible. We're going to work on those. I'll be having a word with your mother about it when I meet her."

"What makes you think you get to meet her?" he teases, tugging my hair softly.

"Well, Ace, I'm going to have to meet her to explain why her son is in the hospital."

"In the hospital?"

"Yes, after I kick you in the face, because I can guarantee it'll take a few times to get you behaving like a well-mannered adult."

"I'm not that bad," he grumbles.

"You scare people. Lena only bakes for you because she's probably scared of you. Give her a smile, maybe a wave." I pause. "Actually, just start with a small wave. If you're too nice to her, she'll think you're crazy and then she'll likely fall and break a hip."

His chest starts shaking. For a moment, I wonder what's happening. One big arm circles my waist, the other slings over my back, and he keeps shaking as he hangs onto me. What the?

I look up, and a huge smile breaks over my face when I see his. Two big dimples greet me, and with those perfect white teeth and eyes so light, they could ignite a whole room. Ace Henderson is laughing, and it's the most beautiful thing I've ever seen in my life.

"I was right," I say to him, my own body starting to shake.

"About what?" he wheezes.

"Your smile, it did stop the world, for just a second."

A beautiful second.

Don't miss these other novels by
USA Today bestselling author
Bella Jewel

THE WATCHER
72 HOURS

From St. Martin's Paperbacks